MUNCLE
TROGG

MUNCLE

Chicken House

SCHOLASTIC INC. / NEW YORK

TROGG

First published in the United Kingdom in 2011 by Chicken House,
2 Palmer Street, Frome, Somerset BA11 1DS.
www.doublecluck.com

Library of Congress Cataloging-in-Publication Data

Foxley, Janet.
Muncle Trogg / by Janet Foxley. — 1st American ed.
p. cm.
Summary: Bullied and despised for being human-sized, a young giant
demonstrates his bravery and cleverness in a series of adventures.
ISBN 978-0-545-37800-0 [1. Giants—Fiction. 2. Size—Fiction.] I. Title.

PZ7.F841225Mu 2012
[Fic]—dc23

2011021233

10 9 8 7 6 5 4 3 2 1   12 13 14 15 16
Printed in the U.S.A.   23

First American edition, March 2012

The text type was set in ITC Stone Informal.

Book design by Whitney Lyle

In memory of my mother, Kitty
1911 – 56

ONE

"Ma!" shrieked Muncle. "Gritt's upside-downing me!"

Muncle tried to wriggle out of his brother's grip.

"Ma!"

He yelled again, swinging wildly. He was going to be sick if Gritt dangled him upside down for much longer.

Ma's fire threw a shadow of a larger-than-life Gritt onto the rocky wall, with a much-too-small Muncle dangling helplessly from his hand. At the age of ten, most giants were nearly full-grown and able to stand up for themselves. But Muncle was far from full-grown and at the moment he couldn't stand up at all. Gritt had him firmly by the ankles. It wouldn't have been so bad if Gritt had been his older brother, but he was younger—three whole *years* younger!

It was a good thing Pa wasn't home yet. He always took Gritt's side. Gritt was the sort of son a giant could be proud of.

Ma Trogg, a handsome giantess with a pleasing number of bristly warts, peered through the cloud of steam above her cauldron.

"Gritt!" she roared. "Put your brother down *right now*!"

"But you told me to play with him till breakfast."

"I didn't mean you should use him as a toy."

"He *likes* it," said Gritt. "Don't you, Muncle?"

"I do *not*!" squealed Muncle.

"Oh. All right. Sorry, Muncle." Gritt dropped his brother as quickly as he'd picked him up.

Muncle might have been small, but at least that made him nimble. The moment Gritt let go, he somer-saulted in midair, landing on his bottom rather than his head.

It still hurt.

Other giants had rolls of comfortable fat and would

have bounced, but Muncle was only skin and bone.

He wasn't bad-looking, though. He had beautiful skin—gray and dotted with hairy warts—Pa's bushy eyebrows and fleshy nose, and Ma's bulging eyes and wonky yellow teeth.

It was just Muncle's size that was wrong. He was simply too small to be a giant.

He'd always struggled to fit in, and now time was running out. The day after tomorrow was his Gigantia final exam. Then he had to find a job. But what sort of job could he do? He was taking only Dragon Science and Smalling Studies—the two subjects that didn't need giant-sized strength—and he knew he wasn't going to do well in either of them.

"We can't wait for your pa any longer or you'll be late for school," said Ma, ladling sticky gray gloop into wooden bowls. "Come and eat your fungus porridge, both of you."

She thumped a large bowl for Gritt and a much smaller one for Muncle onto the low stone table. Ma had given up trying to feed him the same amount as Gritt. Even his appetite was tiny.

She unstrapped Flubb's baby basket from her back

and set Flubb on a stool beside the table. The baby grabbed her leather bottle and glugged eagerly. You could almost see her growing.

Muncle sighed. Life was so unfair. He clambered onto his bracken-filled cushion to help him reach the table, and Ma and Gritt sat on the bare, rocky floor. Then Muncle picked out the best lumps of porridge and arranged them on the table to cool, while Gritt drained the boiling contents of his bowl in one long swig, just like Pa.

Gritt had real talent. At just seven he was already top of the whole school in metalwork. He knew exactly what he wanted to be when he grew up: Chief Weapon-Maker of the King's Armory. There was nothing he didn't know about spears and battle-axes. Pa and Ma thought Gritt was brilliant.

"Seconds!" Gritt demanded.

"Not until Pa's had his," said Ma, getting up and peering into the cauldron. "There might not be enough."

Gritt threw his bowl onto the table. "It's mean of Pa to stay out all night. If he doesn't come home soon, I'll have to go to school *hungry*."

Muncle and Ma looked at each other.

"He'll be all right, Ma," said Muncle. "He's the best hunter in town."

Ma bit her lip. "Raiding isn't the same as hunting, though, is it?" she said. "Stealing a sheep from a Smalling farm isn't like spearing a badger. What if he runs into a Smalling with a magic killing stick?"

Flubb hurled her empty bottle onto the floor and bawled loudly. She was given another helping at once. Well, it was hard to say no to Flubb—she *was* as pretty as a toad.

"No fair!" whined Gritt. "Why should *she* get seconds?"

"Gritt—" Ma began sharply, but at that moment the door of their underground home banged open and Pa tramped into the room with a sack over his shoulder. Bits of twig and leaf were tangled in his long, greasy hair, and his breeches were ripped. Blood dripped from a wound on one of his hairy gray arms.

"Whatever happened to you?" cried Ma, quickly bandaging his arm with a handful of dusty cobwebs.

"Don't fuss, woman. It's nothing. Just a scratch. I had

to take a shortcut through a thicket, that's all."

Pa threw his sack down beside the fire. There was nothing sheep-shaped in it.

"Didn't you get one?" Ma asked anxiously.

"Of course I did. I've already taken it to the palace."

"The King must be bored with sheep for his Birthday supper every year," said Gritt. "You should have brought him a Smalling for a change."

"Gritt," said Pa sternly. "That is not funny." He seized Ma's cauldron straight from the fire and swung it to his lips.

"I wanted seconds!" yelled Gritt.

"Tough luck," said Pa. "Perhaps that'll teach you not to make bad jokes."

Centuries ago, giants had used Smallings as slaves, and sometimes as supper, but that was before they had invented their magic killing sticks and fought back. Now the giants had to live in secret, deep within Mount Grumble. They'd built a whole town in the mountain's old mines.

"It wasn't a joke," said Gritt. "I think we *should* hunt Smallings."

"Gritt!" cried Ma.

"Don't ever let anyone hear you talk like that," said Pa, wiping his rubbery lips on the back of his arm and ending up with a mouthful of cobweb bandage. "You'd be thrown in the dungeons."

"I didn't mean we should have them for every meal," said Gritt. "Not so many that they'd *notice*. Just once a year, on the King's Birthday."

Pa picked bits of cobweb from his beard and ate them with the porridge dregs. "Kidnapping has been against the law for a very long time, as you well know, Gritt Trogg. It's too risky."

"Have *you* been taking risks tonight?" said Ma, frowning. "Is that why you had to take a shortcut through a thicket?"

Pa shrugged. "It was no worse than last year's Birthday raid. A dog barked, but it was a long way off."

"And you came home through the bog, so there was no scent for the dog to follow?"

"I always *do*." Pa took off his boots and emptied them into Ma's cauldron.

Gritt peered into Pa's sack. "Pigeons again," he said with disgust. "Just snacks."

But to Muncle, a pigeon was a meal. Even his breakfast was more than he wanted. "Here, Gritt," he said, "have the rest of my porridge."

"That's hardly a mouthful," his brother said scornfully. "Anyway, I haven't time. I've got to see Titan before school."

"Titan Bulge is in Muncle's class," said Ma. "Why do *you* want to see him?" She ran a hand through her hair, scattering twig hairpins in all directions. Flubb picked one up and chewed on it.

"Gritt wants to be in Titan's gang, Ma," Muncle explained.

The Thunder Thugs were the toughest gang in Mount Grumble with the most daring of entry tests. Thumper Plodd had passed his test by banging the town gong in the middle of the night and waking the Royal Family. There was a rumor that someone had once wrestled a dragon, and that someone else had tried to steal King Thortless's crown.

"It's just lads having fun," Pa told Ma, who was looking anxious. "Titan Bulge is the top in his class, after all. His friends can't be that bad."

"Well . . . ," Muncle began, then thought better of

it. Titan Bulge was the worst bully in the school, and he made Muncle's life a misery, but he didn't want to upset Ma. "I shouldn't worry, he won't get in."

"I will *so* get in," said Gritt, scowling, and he stomped toward the door.

"Wait for me!" Muncle cried, grabbing one of Ma's acorn bread rolls for his lunch as he dashed after his brother. If he walked to school with Gritt, he might not be picked on until he got into his classroom.

"Take care!" shouted Ma.

"I will!" he called back over his shoulder, but how could he, when he was so much smaller than everyone else? It didn't seem fair that Ma still had to worry about him when she had two younger children to look after.

"You shouldn't have told Ma about the Thugs," said Gritt, striding past the guard-dragon stables and into the torchlit street-tunnel.

Muncle scuttled along beside him. "Boys in my class have got into serious trouble in that gang," he told Gritt. "Hefty Clodd spent a month in the dungeons after Titan dared him to shoot a burning arrow through a palace window."

"Well, I'm not going to end up in the dungeons," Gritt said. "I'm not stupid. Come on, Muncle, can't you walk any faster?"

Muncle broke into a jog, and soon they emerged from the shadows into the hazy daylight of the Crater.

The Crater was a huge open-air hollow in the center of Mount Grumble—the only place in the town that was open to the sky. It was the giants' playground, market-place, park, and theater. All the main street-tunnels led to it and the most important buildings were carved into its walls. Here were the shops, the grubhouses, the school, and the King's palace. Smoke from homes and factories trickled from cracks in the Crater wall and merged into the cloud that sat on top of the mountain, hiding the giants and their guard-dragons from the Smallings in the town below.

Muncle felt a pair of enormous hands grab his shoulders, hoisting him into the air.

"Got you!"

It was Titan. He'd been waiting for them.

"Get the string out of my pocket, Gritt," he ordered.

Gritt hung back.

Titan raised his huge bushy eyebrows. "Well, do you want to join the Thunder Thugs or don't you?"

"But he's my broth—"

"You're such a weed, Gritt Trogg," Titan sneered.

This was too much for Muncle. Tormenting *him* was one thing, but taunting his younger brother was quite another, even if he was twice as big. He gathered all his strength and swung his schoolbag straight into Titan's smug face. It was a perfect shot. An enormous zit on the tip of Titan's nose erupted. Blood and pus squirted out in a most spectacular display.

"Yee-ow!" cried Titan. "You'll pay for that, you runtling. I was growing that for the Biggest Boil sideshow at the King's Birthday. Get the string, Gritt. NOW!"

"Um . . . well . . . ," Gritt stammered.

Titan dumped Muncle on the floor, pinning him down with a vast foot, and wrenched out the ropelike string himself. He shoved one end of it through Muncle's belt, tied it in a knot, and began spinning Muncle through the air.

Muncle squeezed his eyes shut and waited for takeoff—but before he could be launched across the Crater, there was a deafening crash. Titan stopped abruptly, and Muncle skidded to a halt in the dust.

He'd been saved by the school gong.

"Got to go," said Gritt. "If I'm late for Dragon Science again, I'll be in trouble with Mr. Thwackum." He threw Muncle a sorry look, then belted across the Crater.

Titan gave Muncle a final punch in the ribs and took off after Gritt, leaving Muncle gasping—and trussed up like a braised badger. Titan was in a hurry, too, and Muncle knew why.

Normally boys like Titan didn't worry about being late. And normally Muncle preferred playing in his den in the forest outside Mount Grumble to going to school at all. But today was not normal. Today was the graduating class's trip, and the whole class had been looking forward to it for weeks—Muncle more than anyone.

They were going to the Smalling world!

TWO

By the time Muncle had untangled himself and reached school, he was late and the door was shut. He was just wondering how he was going to reach the handle when it was helpfully opened from the inside.

Miss Bumfit, the Smalling Studies teacher, scowled down her hooked nose at him. "And who might *you* be?" she demanded.

Muncle felt his face flush purple. His classmates crowded around Miss Bumfit, grinning.

"It's me, Miss. Muncle Trogg."

"Why, so it is. Do you know, it's such a long time

since you've been to a lesson that I'd quite forgotten what you looked like."

The children snickered. They always enjoyed it when the teachers made fun of Muncle, and the teachers made fun of Muncle whenever he went to school. This was why Miss Bumfit hadn't seen much of him.

The rest of the class couldn't wait to get going. They surged forward, sweeping the teacher ahead of them.

Muncle was knocked to the ground by Titan's school-bag. The twins, Colossa and Valkyrie, tripped over him, and Thumper Plodd trod on him. By the time he got up, the others were well ahead and he had to run to catch up with them—and then keep on running, just to *keep* up.

I'm never going to manage this, he thought. *I'll be worn out before we get there.* Pa said it was a long walk through the forest to the cliff top where you could look down on the Smalling town from a safe distance.

But Miss Bumfit brought the class to a halt before they had even left the Crater. They stopped outside a building next to the King's palace. In fact, it was difficult to tell where the palace ended and this building began, which was probably why Muncle had never really noticed it before. Miss Bumfit climbed the steps to the ancient oak door and knocked on it with her teacher's club.

"Now pay attention, class," she said, turning to look down at them. "Before we go in, there are two things to remember. Firstly, this trip is not meant to be *fun*. Part of your Gigantia final exam will be about things you've seen today, so make sure you concentrate."

There was an outbreak of chattering, which Miss Bumfit silenced with a threatening wave of her club.

"Secondly," she said, "remember that everything here belongs to the King, and the whole place is to be treated with the Utmost Respect. What does that mean, Titan?"

"We've got to be careful with everything, Miss."

"Yes, indeed, Titan, and what happens to people who don't treat the King's property with the Utmost Respect?"

"The dungeons, Miss."

"Correct. Now, if we're all ready . . ."

Miss Bumfit knocked on the door again. This time, bolts rattled, locks clattered, and the door creaked slowly open. Inside stood a wrinkled old giant. His skin hung in withered folds, and his back was bent almost in half, so that his beard swept the ground. He leaned heavily on a stick with one hand and, with the other, held an ear trumpet to his ear.

"This is His Wiseness Sir Biblos," said Miss Bumfit, "the most important person in Mount Grumble after the Royal Family. He is Wise Man of the Council, Royal Museum Master, and Keeper of the Book."

"The Wise Man is the King's chief adviser," the old man explained. He pushed aside his beard to show them his golden chain of office. "When the King needs a good idea, it's my job to give him one. Another of my duties is to look after this wonderful Museum of the Smalling World."

"Why is he so wrinkly?" whispered Valkyrie.

"It's what happens when you think too much," said Thumper.

The children rushed up the steps—all but Muncle, who was so disappointed he felt as if he'd been bashed on the head by Miss Bumfit's club.

They weren't going to see the Smalling world at all. They were just going to look around some stuffy old museum. Muncle hadn't been in class when they'd been told about the trip, and he must have misheard when the other children talked about it. It hadn't been worth coming to school today after all.

He wondered whether anyone would notice if he crept quietly away, but then he remembered the Gigantia final exam. This visit might just make up for all his missed Smalling Studies lessons. He'd better go.

He sighed and dragged himself up the steps to join the others.

The Wise Man was moving around the museum, pointing out objects that had been stolen from Smallings in the days when they were kidnapped, but Muncle couldn't see anything, because he was in the back, behind the normal-sized children.

"And now," Sir Biblos was saying, "we come to the display that makes it clear how tiny Smallings really are."

Muncle heard a door creak open. Everyone crowded forward.

"So," said Sir Biblos, "what do you think these things are?"

"Baby clothes?" Valkyrie suggested.

"No," said Sir Biblos. "These are the clothes of a grown-up Smalling, the last one ever kidnapped."

"Oooh!" gasped the class.

"Oooh, indeed," agreed Biblos. "It's hard to imagine anyone tiny enough to wear them, isn't it?"

"Muncle Trogg could fit into them, with room to spare!" Titan laughed.

"Muncle Trogg?" said Sir Biblos. "Who is Muncle Trogg?"

"*Where* is Muncle Trogg?" said Miss Bumfit. "Is he missing again?"

Usually Muncle found it safer to keep quiet, but now he was curious to see what everyone else was looking at.

"I'm here," he said, as loudly as he could.

The other children turned toward him. Hands reached out and grabbed him, then lifted him overhead. It was a rough way to travel, but not as rough as being a plaything, and it didn't last long. He was passed forward quickly and dumped in front of Sir Biblos.

"A first year?" exclaimed the old man. "But this visit is for fifth-year students only, Miss Bumfit."

"And Muncle Trogg is just that," said Miss Bumfit. "He's been in school for the full five years. He has a younger brother who is perfectly normal."

"Dear me," said Sir Biblos, looking down at him. "You poor boy."

He pulled up a footstool and sat down on it to study Muncle more closely.

"Your friend's right," he said. "I think these clothes *would* fit you. Try them on. We'll all get a better idea of what a Smalling looks like if we see someone wearing them."

Muncle eagerly peeled off his tattered jerkin. He loved pretending to be a Smalling! Often, when people were giving him a really hard time, he would imagine that he didn't belong in Mount Grumble at all, that he really *was* a Smalling, swapped by fairies for Ma and Pa's real son. That was just the sort of thing fairies did. (Except that fairies weren't around anymore. They'd disappeared ages ago, along with the dwarfs and the elves.)

The shirt Sir Biblos gave him was almost thin enough to see through. He drew it over his head carefully, afraid that such fine material would tear, but it was stronger than it looked.

As he pulled the shirt down over the top of his breeches, Muncle suddenly thought of the last person to wear it. A Smalling had been captured by a giant in these clothes, and might even have died a grizzly death. He examined the shirt for bloodstains, and was glad he couldn't see any. Giants were supposed to love violence, but Muncle had spent too much time getting beaten up to enjoy that sort of thing.

"Now these."

The soft woolen breeches were about the same length as his own, but they buttoned below the knee instead of hanging straight. They were much easier to move in than the stiff, scratchy string-cloth ones the giants wore.

Next, Sir Biblos handed him two knitted tubes. Puzzled, Muncle pushed his arm into one.

"No, no, Muncle. On your *feet*. They are called 'socks.' And you put these on top."

"Boots!"

Muncle was thrilled. The boots were heavy but they made him feel just like Pa. Hunters and gatherers were the only giants who wore boots, as it made it harder for dogs to pick up their scent.

"Tuck the shirt into your breeches, Muncle, and you'll be ready for the waistcoat."

The waistcoat was like a jerkin, but with tiny

buttons. It took Muncle ages to wriggle them into their buttonholes.

"Extraordinary," Sir Biblos declared as he tied a square of thin red cloth around Muncle's neck to complete the outfit. "Quite extraordinary. I never expected to see a Smalling come to life before my very eyes."

"It's not a Smalling," sneered Titan. "It's just Muncle Trogg in silly clothes. This is boring. When are we going to see the Book?"

THREE

"Yes! We want the Book! We want the Book!" shouted the rest of the class.

Muncle had no idea what "the Book" was. Probably something they'd learned about on one of his "days off."

"The Book is our most important exhibit," said Sir Biblos proudly, "which is why I've kept it till last. Get it out, please, Muncle."

"What?"

"You know where it is, don't you?"

Muncle shook his head.

"Well, we keep it, for safety, exactly where we found it. Miss Bumfit must have taught you *that*."

Oh, no! Was he going to have to admit that he didn't know anything Miss Bumfit had taught? Amazingly, he was saved by Titan, who clearly wanted to show off.

"In your pocket!" he yelled.

That couldn't be right. His clothes felt much too light to have anything important in their pockets. But Sir Biblos was smiling and nodding. Muncle felt all around, and at the back of his breeches he found a pocket fastened with a button. He fumbled with it, and pulled out a flat object covered in black animal skin. It was roughly square in shape and no bigger than the palm of his hand. Could this really be what all the fuss was about?

"Look inside," said Sir Biblos. "Carefully. Inside are 'pages' and they are made of something called 'paper.' They're as fragile as winter leaves."

Gently, Muncle opened the Book. At the top of each page was a row of clear, separate symbols. Below them, the marks looked different—looping, wriggling lines. It was impossible to know what any of it meant. Muncle couldn't see what there was to get excited about.

He looked at Sir Biblos. The Wise Man beamed back.

"There," he said, "I bet you never thought you'd hold the Smallings' Book of Magic in your own hands, did you?"

Muncle gasped. *"Magic?"*

"Yeah, magic," said Titan, barging to the front and reaching for the Book.

Sir Biblos barred his way with a surprisingly forceful swing of his ear trumpet. "No one but Muncle is to touch it," he said. "The Book is safer in his tiny hands than in any of ours."

"But if we've had the Smallings' magic all this time," Muncle said thoughtfully, "how come we're still frightened of them?"

Titan scowled at him for a few moments. Then his forehead slowly unfolded. "Yeah," he said. "Why can't we go back to having Smalling slaves to do our work for us? Why can't we go back to *kidnapping*?"

"I'm afraid it's not that easy," said Sir Biblos. "You see, although we've *found* the magic, the Smallings haven't *lost* it. They must have more books. Perhaps everyone's got one."

"But that doesn't matter," said Muncle. "If we've *both*

got magic, they'll cancel each other out and we'll be able to win again, because giants will always be stronger than Smallings."

"Not all of them!" said Titan, and he picked Muncle up and tossed him over his shoulder like a sack of pigeons. Everyone laughed, except Sir Biblos, who rescued Muncle and put him back on his feet.

"If only you were right, Muncle," he said with a sigh. "We could live in the outside world again. We'd feel the sun on our backs, and grow crops that need sunlight. Fungus is very good for us, so we shouldn't complain, but it's a pity there's nothing else we can grow underground. It must have been wonderful in the old days, when we could live wherever we liked. But you see, although we've *got* this magic, we can't use it. We can't understand the marks and symbols. We can't read."

"But you're His *Wiseness* the *Wise* Man," said Titan.

"Titan Bulge, detention!" snapped Miss Bumfit. "How dare you be rude to the most important person in Mount Grumble after the Royal Family?"

"No, no, Miss Bumfit, the boy's right. I *am* the Wise Man. I *ought* to be able to read, but I can't. I'm not wise *enough.* And nor were any of the Wise Men before me."

"The Book's not much good, then, is it?" said Muncle, looking with interest at the rows of wriggling lines.

"Not at the moment," said Sir Biblos, "but perhaps one day we'll have a Wise Man who *can* read. Perhaps one day we *will* be able to take our place in the outside world once again."

At that moment, the Crater echoed to the sound of the King's Timekeeper striking the midday gong.

"Food!" the children bellowed. They rushed outside, all thoughts of Smalling magic forgotten. Miss Bumfit thanked Sir Biblos and hurried after them. The trip was over.

Muncle buttoned the Book safely into its pocket, and reluctantly took off the Smalling clothes.

"You'd better be quick," said Sir Biblos, "or there'll be no food left."

"Oh, no," said Muncle. "I don't have school lunches. I've got a roll in my bag."

Sir Biblos looked at him kindly. "Well, if you're in no hurry, I'd like to have a chat with you. And I think we can do better than a roll. We'll go to the grubhouse next door and you can have whatever you like."

Muncle stared at him. What could the Wise Man possibly want to chat to him about? "Are you sure you haven't got something more important to do?" he asked.

"More important than having lunch?" said Sir Biblos. "Certainly not." He gathered up the Smalling clothes and folded them into a parcel. "Here, you carry these," he said. "You can put them in your schoolbag. I need both hands for my stick and ear trumpet."

"But why are we taking them with us?" Muncle asked.

"You'll see," said the Wise Man. "I've got an idea."

MuckGristle's was the fanciest place to eat in Mount Grumble. It was beautifully decorated with the parts of animals that the cook threw out. There were bone candlesticks on every table, and the walls were covered in skins. Three badgers were roasting on a spit in front of the fire and the air was filled with a mouthwatering smell of burnt fat.

Nervously, Muncle looked at the other customers. There was Nugsnatch the banker, Gobbitt the doctor, and Sleazewig the judge—all important people who earned a hundred or more nuggets a month.

Sir Biblos sank onto a chair of gnarled wood under a fox-skin wall-hanging. "Sit down, Muncle. Now, what would you like?"

"What is there?" asked Muncle, who'd never been in a grubhouse before. He struggled up onto one of the huge chairs and perched on the edge.

Sir Biblos clearly ate there every day, because he knew the menu without having to ask.

"Fox fingers and fir-cones," he said, "squirrels-on-a-skewer, ditchwater broth, badger burgers, or crunchy hedgehog pie. If you want something lighter, I can recommend the slugs-on-toast. You'll want to leave room for dessert. The frogspawn crumble is delicious."

"Squirrel, please. Just the one." Muncle had eaten squirrel at home and knew it was something he liked.

It didn't take long for the food to come. It was nicely dry and black—just right.

"Sir Biblos . . . ," said Muncle as he gnawed his squirrel's tail.

"Just Biblos, please," said the old man. "Once upon a time I felt proud of all my titles, but nowadays they just seem to weigh me down."

"Biblos," Muncle began again, "do you really think there might one day be a Wise Man who could do it? Who could read the Book and use the magic, so we didn't have to hide from the Smallings anymore? I mean, how *do* you learn to read?"

Biblos sighed. "If I knew that," he said, "I'd have done it myself. I've stared and stared at those symbols over the years, but I still can't make any sense of them. I sometimes think the only way to learn would be to get a Smalling to teach me."

"But that's impossible."

"Quite. Still, we don't have a bad life here, do we?"

Speak for yourself, thought Muncle.

Biblos sensed his thought. "That boy who threw you over his shoulder . . ."

"Titan Bulge."

"He treats you like that all the time?"

"They all do."

The Wise Man looked thoughtful. "Muncle, I think I know a way for you to earn some respect—and some money, of course."

"Really?"

Respect would be good. And, since he was about to

leave school with no job, money would be even better.

"Really," Biblos continued. "Now, it was so interesting to see you dressed up as a Smalling this morning that I thought the whole town ought to see it."

"What? How?"

"In the Burps 'n' Farts competition at the King's Birthday Party."

"But I can't burp twenty times in a row or fart louder than a dragon's roar!"

"You don't have to. Nowadays the competition is much wider than that—fire-eating, sword-swallowing, anything that will amuse the King. You'd just dress up in the Smalling clothes, and walk up and down on the stage."

Muncle frowned. "But what if people think I'm a *real* Smalling? What if they throw me to the dragons? What if they *roast* me? I don't want to end up on the King's plate."

"I'll be there to see there are no mistakes," Biblos promised.

Muncle couldn't wait to wear the Smalling clothes again, but he wasn't sure King Thortless would find walking up and down very amusing.

"What if we made it into a play?" he said. "I could be a Smalling fighting a giant king. The king would win, of course."

"Brilliant!" Biblos stared at Muncle. "Why didn't I think of that? King Thortless will love it."

"And if the Smalling had a killing stick," Muncle went on, "the king would look even more powerful when he beats him."

"Ah." Biblos shook his head. "I'm afraid there are no killing sticks in the museum."

"Couldn't I just use an ordinary stick and pretend it was a magic one?"

Biblos's jaw dropped open to show a half-chewed bite of badger burger. "You really *are* brilliant," he said. "Of course you could. Now, we'll have to choose someone to play the part of the king, someone who wouldn't really hurt you. What about your pa?"

"I don't know. Acting's not exactly his thing."

"Not even for a prize of fifty nuggets?"

How much? Pa would do *anything* for fifty nuggets. Fifty nuggets was more than he earned in three months, even though he had two jobs. The Troggs were one of the poorest families in Mount Grumble. They couldn't even afford a guard-dragon. Until Gritt had been born, the neighbors used to joke that Ma and Pa couldn't afford a full-sized child.

"He'll do it," said Muncle firmly. This was so exciting! There simply couldn't be a better act than a giant king beating a Smalling in battle. They were bound to win.

"Excellent," said Biblos. "Now, are you ready for some of that frogspawn crumble?"

"Are you sure? It must be very expensive."

"The King pays," said Biblos, and when they'd eaten their crumble and the one-eyed waitress came for their money, all he did was wave the badge on his chain of office and she nodded and let them go.

"What *is* that on your chain?" asked Muncle as they made their way back to the museum.

"This?" Biblos held up the gold badge. On it was a picture of a strange-looking, long-eared animal. "It's my sacred donkey badge. It's a symbol of wisdom and it shows that I'm a Wise Man. The donkey is the smartest creature on earth and the only one you must never eat. Didn't they teach you that at school?"

"Er . . . yes," said Muncle. This was another lesson

he must have missed. "I just didn't know what it looked like. Thank you very much for my nice lunch. I promise I'll look after the Smalling clothes."

"I'm sure you will," said Biblos. "I knew at once you were someone I could trust. Now, you must keep your act secret. It'll be much more exciting if it's a surprise. Don't put on the Smalling clothes until the competition begins—there'll be a space under the stage where you can get changed. And remember, you've only got two days to practice."

"We'll start this afternoon," said Muncle.

"Splendid," said Biblos, bending his already bent form to pat Muncle on the shoulder. "Most giants have no idea what a Smalling really looks like, you know. This King's Birthday is going to be one to remember."

FOUR

Biblos shuffled back into the museum, and Muncle hurried off in search of Pa. After his night's hunting he'd have slept all morning and would now be at his part-time job at the Dragon Farm. That would be a much safer place to tell him about the King's Birthday act than at home with the whole family listening. Gritt could spread a secret around Mount Grumble faster than the Town Crier.

There were lots of good jobs at the Dragon Farm, like keeping the eggs warm if the mother dragons didn't do it properly, or feeding, grooming, and training the babies until they were big enough to be sold as guard-dragons. But Pa didn't have one of the good jobs. Pa was a mucker-out.

Muncle walked past the cages of dragons in the farm shop and wished they could afford to buy one. Here were the Common Red and Green varieties that they had at school, but also the rarer and much more expensive Purple Nobles and Rainbow Royals. He put out a hand to stroke the most handsome of all the Royals, ready to snatch it back if the dragon shot flames at him. It didn't. The Royal sniffed his hand with interest, then licked the remains of Muncle's squirrel meal off his fingers.

It tickled, and Muncle laughed.

"Hey, you!" shouted a shop assistant. "Get away from that cage. No touching unless you're buying. What are you doing here anyway? No children allowed in the Dragon Farm on their own."

"I'm not on my own," said Muncle. "I'm with my pa. He's working downstairs."

"Then get downstairs yourself, and don't leave your pa again."

Muncle tramped down the stone stairs to where Pa worked, deep in the bowels of the mountain among the two- and three-year-old dragons. He loved it down here, even though the pong of dragon pee stung his eyes and throat. There was no fire, but for some reason it was always hot and smoky. He supposed it must be due to keeping so many dragons in a small space. And it was as secret as you could get. No one but Pa was there in the afternoons.

"Muncle?" said Pa, who was busy mopping up dragon pee. "Why aren't you at school?"

"The trip ended early and they let us go straight home," lied Muncle, who was an expert in explaining his time off from school. He hopped from one foot to the other on the scorching floor. "And guess what, Pa—I had lunch with the Wise Man, at MuckGristle's!"

"Muncle, your jokes are even worse than Gritt's." Pa wiped the sweat from his face, then wrung out the mop with his massive hands. Steaming yellow liquid squirted into his bucket.

"It's not a joke, honestly. Look, he lent me these...."

Muncle pulled off his own clothes, hung them over a dragon cage to keep them off the floor, and put on the Smalling ones. He could tell at once what a good idea boots were. They kept his feet off the hot floor and out of the pee puddles.

"You look ridiculous."

"I look like a Smalling."

"You should be trying to look more like a *giant*. Why the thrumbles do you want to look like a Smalling?"

"So I can win fifty nuggets. Well, you and me together."

"What?"

Muncle explained. Three times.

"You mean I'd be the hero?" said Pa, when he'd got it at last. "In front of the King and the whole town?" He put down his mop and bucket. "Come here, lad, let's have a go right away." He grabbed Muncle by the hair and threw him across the stables.

"Steady, Pa!" cried Muncle, landing in a puddle.

"Don't tell me that tiny bounce hurt you?"

It had, but Muncle didn't complain. The fight would have to look real to win the prize.

"It's the clothes I'm worried about." He gasped as Pa twirled him over his head. "They're the King's property. Miss Bumfit said we have to treat them with the Utmost Respect."

Pa tossed Muncle from his left hand to his right. "Don't worry. Ma can always wash them."

"*What?*"

Pa tossed Muncle from his right hand to his left. "I said Ma can wash them."

"*Wash* them?"

Muncle bounced off Pa's hand and somersaulted to the floor.

"Yes. She washed mine once, when I fell over in a field and came home smelling all sweet and flowery and horrible."

"All right, but I still think we ought to stop, before we tear them. You're a very good actor, Pa. We can do it. I don't think we need to practice anymore. And, Pa, remember: This has to be a secret. If I go home now, I'll have time to tell Ma all about it before Gritt gets in. Ma can keep a secret, and Flubb won't tell anyone, because she can only say 'Ma' and 'Pa' and 'Mumble' and 'Git.'"

"I want to tell her, too," said Pa. "I'll finish up here and knock off early. No one will ever know."

While Muncle changed back into his own clothes, Pa quickly swept the floods of dragon pee down the cracks in the rocky floor.

"Are you allowed to do that?" asked Muncle. "I thought it all had to be given to the King's Treasury for turning into gold."

"They only collect it once a month," said Pa. "They won't notice if there's a bit missing."

As they reached home, Pa and Muncle realized that they were too late. Gritt had got home ahead of them.

"Why aren't you at school?" said Pa. "*You* didn't have a class trip today."

Gritt sat huddled in a corner, his knees drawn up to his chin. He avoided Pa's eyes and said nothing.

"You've got to tell him, Gritt," said Ma, stirring her cauldron. By the smell of it, supper was stewed pigeons in nettle sauce.

"Tell me what?" demanded Pa.

"I've been expelled," muttered Gritt.

"*Expelled?*" said Muncle, dropping his bag on the floor. "What the bloggus did you do?"

Gritt had been sent home once before, when Titan had dared him to give a school dragon a drink of water. Its fire had gone right out and the poor creature had been ill for weeks. What could he possibly have done that was worse than that?

"I lost a dragon," Gritt admitted, in what for him was a very small voice.

Pa buried his head in his hands. "Chundering chilbugs, Gritt!" he said.

"How did you manage to lose him?" asked Muncle.

"We've only ever done grooming and mucking out before," Gritt said. "But today Mr. Thwackum said it was time we did feeding, so we took the dragons onto the mountainside for their daily drink of sunshine. Only it was cloudy, so we left them to wait for the sun to come out, and went to our next class."

"You often have to do that. You just fetch them back later."

"We did, Pa. But Snarg wasn't there."

"So what are you doing at home?" growled Pa. "You should be out there looking for him."

"Let's all go and look for him," said Muncle. "Pa's got a hunters' key for the town gates. He can let us all out. Dragons are slow on land, so he can't have wandered far."

"He didn't wander at all," said Gritt wretchedly.

"He flew. I saw him. We all saw him. Mr. Thwackum saw him."

"Impossible!" roared Pa. "The two most important facts about guard-dragons are they can't be ridden and they can't fly."

"But he *did* fly, Pa. I must have forgotten to clip his wings last week."

"Oh, Gritt," said Ma. "You've been grooming that dragon all term. How could you possibly have forgotten?"

"You just can't keep damaging school property like this!" Pa groaned.

"Actually, I think he was *un*damaged," said Muncle. "Surely it's *clipping* their wings that damages them?"

"What would you know?" snapped Pa. "You've never handled a dragon."

This was all too true. Muncle was paired with Brutus Lunk for Dragon Science, and Brutus did all the practical work. He'd never even let Muncle groom the dragon bits he could reach. Muncle would have loved to feed the school dragon and polish its scales, but he'd never wanted to clip its wings. He'd seen the fear in the animal's eyes whenever the dragon shears were produced. Clipping must hurt.

"Never mind, Gritt," said Ma. "School isn't every-thing. We'll find you a job instead."

"Not the sort of job I want," moaned Gritt, and some-thing that looked very like a tear traced a clean path down his grimy cheek.

"With no Gigantia passes, he'd do no better in life than Muncle," added Pa. "He wouldn't get a job making cooking pots, let alone battle-axes. I'm not having *both* my sons letting me down. We've got to get him back into school somehow."

"Well," said Ma, "I'm sure if we bought another dragon . . ."

"*Bought* one?" Pa spluttered. "What with? A well-trained dragon costs fifty nuggets. Where do you expect me to find that kind of money?"

"But you *know* where, Pa," Muncle whispered.

"Ha!" Pa didn't know how to whisper. "I'm not wasting that money buying another dragon when Gritt shouldn't have lost the school one in the first place."

"What money?" Gritt began to cheer up.

"Don't worry, Gritt," said Muncle. "We'll soon be able to afford a Common Red."

"Snarg was a Common Green."

"Even better. They're the cheapest of all."

"What are you talking about?" said Ma. "Where do you think this money is suddenly going to come from?"

"I can't tell you just yet," said Muncle, rolling his eyes toward his brother, trying to tell Ma that he wanted to keep a secret from Gritt, not from her. "But trust me, in a couple of days everything will be all right."

FIVE

Muncle wriggled about in his bed, trying to find places where the lumps in his bracken mattress didn't dig in to his bruises. Pa really had thrown him around hard today. Then he started to think about the Smalling clothes. He'd packed them up so quickly at the Dragon Farm, he hadn't checked to see if they'd been torn.

Soon his thinking turned to worrying.

Once Pa had gone out hunting and the kitchen echoed with the snores of Ma, Gritt, and Flubb, he pulled his curtain aside and crawled out of his bedroom hole.

He sneaked over to the embers of Ma's fire, and lit a stub of candle.

Safely back behind his curtain, he took the Smalling clothes out of his schoolbag one by one. They weren't quite the color they'd been before, and they didn't smell quite the same as before, either, but there were no rips and none of the buttons had come off and . . . Blistering bogspots! The Book! All the time Pa had been throwing him around like a dead sheep, the Book had been in his pocket—and it was as fragile as winter leaves! Had Biblos forgotten it was there when he lent him the clothes?

Muncle fumbled with the pocket button and fished it out. It looked all right. The animal-skin cover must have protected it. *Phew.* As he carefully checked the pages, he began to notice that most of the symbols cropped up again and again. They were quite simple shapes, not hard to copy. He traced them on the dusty floor with his finger.

T—that was easy.

R—the curved line was a bit harder.

E—straight lines, easier again.

He was writing!

But he wasn't reading. He had no idea how to make any of these magic spells happen.

The candle's flame wavered. Muncle slipped the Book back into its pocket and folded the clothes away in his bag before the light flickered out. Then he lay down in the darkness and began to wonder.

Could he?

Dare he?

He MUST!

He was the only giant who could disguise himself in Smalling clothes. He had to be the one to go to the Smalling town and find out how to read.

It was still early when Muncle stopped trying to sleep, but he didn't get up until he heard Pa come home and go to bed. It was best to keep away from Pa in the morning because he was always tired and grumpy. The door banged again as Muncle crawled out of his bedroom hole. Gritt clearly wanted to avoid Pa, too.

Ma was putting on her makeup by the fire. Flubb sat on the floor trying to copy her. She reached into the fire for a blackened twig, then poked herself in the eye with it. She howled. But even she was tougher than Muncle, who couldn't have put his hand in the fire without getting burned.

"No, my precious Flubb-a-lub," said Ma, hugging her. "You draw *around* your eye with the twig, like this. Hello, Muncle. You're up early. Not as early as Gritt, mind. He's gone out already." She looked anxious. "I hope he's not meeting Titan again. But if there's something you're keeping secret from him, now's the time to tell me. What's all this about being able to pay for a new dragon?"

Muncle explained about the Burps 'n' Farts competition.

"Don't go dropping any hints to Gritt," he added, "or it'll be all over town. But don't worry, we'll get him back in school."

Ma hugged him. "I always knew you being small would come in useful one day," she said, smiling.

Breakfast was the usual fungus porridge, mixed with the leftovers from last night's pigeon stew. Muncle was too excited to eat. He was about to go on an adventure that could be dangerous and was definitely against the law. Eating now would make him sick, and he didn't want to go on an adventure feeling ill. Feeling frightened was bad enough. Instead, he squeezed an extra acorn bread roll into his bag with the Smalling clothes.

"You off already?" said Ma. "You'll be early for school."

"There's a practice exam class before assembly," Muncle fibbed.

"Oh, well, you mustn't miss that. Take care."

"I will," said Muncle, just as he always did.

But if he ran into trouble today, it wouldn't come from school bullies and spiteful teachers.

Long ago, when the giants had lived in the outdoors and kidnapped Smallings, the Smallings had started to fight back with machines on wheels that threw balls of stone. They weren't a problem. The giants simply caught the balls and threw them back.

But then the machines changed. They breathed fire like dragons, and the balls they threw exploded, killing whoever caught them. Later came the killing sticks, light enough to be carried by a single Smalling. They breathed fire, too, and spat out metal acorns that could tear through a giant's flesh like an ax through sand.

That was when the giants had moved into Mount Grumble, building gates at the openings of all the old mine tunnels to keep the Smallings out. But that had been centuries ago. The Smallings seemed to have forgotten where the giants had hidden, and the giants had forgotten to repair some of the gates. Muncle had found a rusty one with a hole in it. This was how he got out of Mount Grumble when he wanted to escape the bullying. And it was how he got out today.

The gate was covered with brambles and ivy, and Muncle had to fight his way through, but after a few moments he stepped out into the forest. He shivered. It was chilly outside the warm mountain, but he loved everything here—the rippling of the stream, the wisps of mist winding between the trees, and, above all, the lack of bullies.

He followed the stream the short distance to his secret den. The old hut in the clearing must have belonged to Smallings once—he knew that from its size—but he'd never felt afraid here. Smallings hadn't been seen in the forest in living memory. And even if he did happen to bump into one, he was sure they'd think he was just another Smalling. Especially now that he had the proper clothes.

As he changed into them, he tried to picture the town he was about to visit. Would it be a cluster of wooden huts like this one, all huddled around an outside cooking fire? It might not be safe to cook indoors if you lived in a wooden house. Would he get a chance to look inside a Smalling house?

He squeezed his acorn bread rolls into the spare pockets in the museum breeches, and hid his school-bag and his string-cloth clothes in the corner of the hut under a pile of dead leaves.

He was ready.

Although Muncle had never been farther than this hut before, he'd heard Pa talk about the forest so often that he felt he knew it well.

To reach the Smalling town, you just follow the stream to the foot of the mountain.

It sounded easy enough. But it wasn't, if you weren't very brave.

It wouldn't have been quite so scary if Pa had warned him about the noises. Muncle knew there were no wolves or bears left—hunters had caught the last of those ages ago—but as he padded along beside the stream it was easy to believe there was something big and dangerous lurking around, with all that rustling and cracking in the undergrowth.

"Deer," he said out loud, trying to convince himself. "Deer are shy animals. Pa's never managed to catch one. A deer won't hurt me."

The forest was growing more and more spooky the farther down the mountain he went. The cloud was thin here, and brightness that he knew must be sunshine filtered between the branches, setting the shadows of twigs and leaves dancing on the ground. It felt as if the forest itself was coming to life.

He stopped, his heart thumping fast and loud.

"Calm down," he whispered. "This is actually less dangerous than going to school. No one's going to hurt you today. The Smallings won't bully you, because in *their* town you won't be different. And they won't take you for a giant in these clothes. So what is there to be afraid of?"

He took a deep breath and carried on.

At the bottom of the mountain, there were fewer trees. All trace of cloud had vanished, melted away by a dazzling sun. Like Gritt, Muncle had only ever been out to the dragon feeding station when the sun was hidden by cloud. He had no idea the world could be this bright. Blinded, he clamped his eyes shut, then squinted at the view fuzzily, through his eyelashes.

The stream he'd been following plunged under a low arch, and disappeared. And ahead of him was a fence as tall as he was. It wouldn't keep a giant out of the town. It wouldn't even keep a Smalling out of the forest. But it did mark the beginning of the Smalling world.

He'd arrived.

SIX

Muncle shaded his eyes with his hands. Then he opened them wider. What he saw above the fence amazed him.

Houses as tall as giants, with sloping roofs and smoking boxes on top!

He edged alongside the fence until a noise like the purring of a well-fed dragon tempted him to stand on tiptoe and peep over the top. The purring thing was a machine. It was biting off the grass and spitting it into a box. Behind it, and holding on to it with both hands, walked a man.

His first Smalling! What the bloggus was he doing?

Muncle wished the sun wasn't quite so bright. It really made it very hard to see. The man was wearing a shirt quite like Muncle's, but he had strangely short arms, and the sleeves reached all the way to his wrists. His legs looked normal, but his breeches reached all the way to his ankles.

A little worry began to nag at the back of Muncle's mind. He ducked back behind the fence and crept along a bit farther. Then he peeped over again.

This time he saw a metal tree, its straight branches draped with shiny yellow string. For some reason, a Smalling was pinning clothes to it. He thought it must be a woman, even though she was wearing ankle-length breeches, too, because she had a sort of bosom.

Muncle dipped back down, thought about it for a moment, and then had another look. Yes, it had to be a bosom. But it was in a funny place. It stuck out high up in front, instead of sitting comfortably on top of the woman's belly, like Ma's.

Muncle's nagging worry grew.

He followed the fence until it turned a corner, leading him to an alley between two rows of houses. The sun threw the shadow of the houses halfway across the alley. Muncle shrank into them. That was better. He was used to hiding in the street-tunnel shadows at home. Now he could open his eyes properly.

He had taken only three steps down the alley when another Smalling came out of a gate and strode away without looking in Muncle's direction. He was about Muncle's height, but his back was as straight as a tree trunk and his knuckles didn't even reach his knees.

Muncle dared not go a step farther.

Either these Smallings all had a funny disease . . . or Muncle didn't look like a Smalling at all.

Before he could back away, the gate clicked again and a second Smalling came out. This one was tiny. Muncle guessed she was a child. She was wearing a thick woolly shirt and a funny little skirt that didn't reach her knees. Below it, her legs were as smooth as her face, with no trace of bristles. She had a sprinkling of tiny brown dots instead of warts across her upturned nose. Her long yellow hair shone like nuggets, and was bunched together with a blue ribbon so that it hung down her back like the tail of a golden fox.

Even if Muncle's clothes had been right, even if

his back had been straight and his arms shorter, the Smallings would never have taken him for one of their own. His gray, warty skin alone would have given him away.

"Hurry up, Emily!" called the man as he disappeared around a corner. "You don't want to be late."

But Emily had seen Muncle and was staring at him with her mouth open.

He had to think quickly. Running away would look suspicious. He'd better be friendly.

"Good morning," he said, with his broadest yellow-toothed smile.

Emily stopped staring and smiled back. Her teeth were even and very white.

"Oh," she said. "I didn't know if you spoke English. You're here with the circus, aren't you?"

Muncle had no idea what a circus was, so he just smiled again.

"Mom and Dad are taking me tonight," said Emily. "I'm really looking forward to it, especially the clowns. I've never seen one made up quite like you before. I bet you're really funny."

Muncle still hadn't a clue what she was talking

about, but he could tell she was being nice. Now was his chance.

"Can you help me?" he said, fishing the Book out of his pocket. "I'm looking for someone who can read."

Emily looked startled. "Didn't you have lessons when you were little? I'd like to help, but I can't stop now or I'll be late for school. Sorry. Bye!"

She smiled again, then turned and ran down the alley, her yellow fox-tail bouncing up and down on her straight back.

She'd just thought he was funny. She hadn't realized he was a giant! Muncle felt much better. He followed Emily to the wide road at the end of the alley in search of someone else who might help him.

Whoosh.

As he came out into the sunshine again, a cart whizzed past at unbelievable speed. It only just missed him.

Pa had told him about metal carts that moved by themselves, but Muncle hadn't thought they'd be so terrifying. He found he was shaking.

Whoosh. Whoosh.

He didn't like them one bit.

"Hey, you!"

Frozen by the sight of the speeding carts, Muncle hadn't seen two Smallings approaching on foot. They both wore bright yellow jerkins over dark blue clothes.

"You shouldn't be in this part of town!" one of them shouted. "Not after the trouble you caused last year. You know the rules. You're supposed to stay on your circus campsite."

Muncle didn't know what they were talking about, but he had a feeling these weren't the right people to ask about reading. They seemed much more like the dangerous Smallings he'd been told about. Then the other Smalling pulled out a stick—a killing stick!—and broke into a run.

Muncle broke into a run, too.

Back up the alley, back along the fence, back through the forest.

He didn't stop running until he reached his secret den, where he collapsed on the ground by the stream, so out of breath it hurt. Only then did he realize he should have run in the other direction to lead the Smallings *away* from Mount Grumble!

Apart from the rippling of the water and a few bird calls, it was quiet in the clearing. Bit by bit, Muncle's thumping heart slowed. The burning in his chest began to ease. His hands stopped shaking. Those men with the killing sticks would have been here by now if they'd seen which way he went. It was all right. He was safe. And so was Mount Grumble.

He was so relieved he almost cried. It didn't matter that he wasn't going home a hero who could read magic spells. All he cared about was that the giants were still safe in their mountain.

He reached out to scoop a drink from the stream, and realized he was still holding the Book. He shoved it back into his pocket, unread.

Learning to read was just a stupid dream, he told himself. *But at least I've learned something today: I've learned what Smallings are really like.*

He felt sad, knowing he couldn't pretend he was a Smalling dropped by fairies into the giants' world anymore, but then he cheered up a bit. At least he'd be able to surprise Miss Bumfit by how much he knew about Smallings. He would definitely pass the Smalling Studies exam now. It was a pity he couldn't catch up on all the

Dragon Science he'd missed as well, but one pass was better than none.

He nibbled an acorn bread roll, washing it down with a nice drink of muddy water. Then he changed into his own clothes and put the others back in his bag, making sure the Book was safely buttoned into the breeches pocket.

Taking his time, he headed for home—Ma would be suspicious if he got back before school finished.

Crack. Rustle.

Rustle. Crack.

Muncle stopped and held his breath.

Rustle. Rustle.

He let it out again. There was no need to be scared. It was that deer, he was sure of it. After his escape from a Smalling with a killing stick, Muncle was not going to be frightened by a harmless animal.

Treading as softly as he could, he gently parted the undergrowth. Now he could make out something moving.

Not a deer.

A light.

The Smallings were looking for him after all.

SEVEN

Muncle needed to hide, and quickly. He burrowed into the undergrowth, but as he moved, a second light appeared.

Two flaming orange lights, close together.

They went out and immediately came on again.

There was only one sort of flaming orange lights that blinked. And they didn't belong to a deer.

"Snarg," he said softly, "what are you doing down here? Why aren't you up above the clouds, in the sun?"

The lost school dragon pushed his way through the

undergrowth toward him with an unhappy whimper. He didn't sound fierce at all.

"What's the matter, boy?" said Muncle. "You've got your freedom. What more do you want?"

Then he saw. Not used to having a full wingspan, Snarg had somehow managed to catch his left wing in his collar.

"Does it hurt?" asked Muncle. He stretched out his hand, but the collar was way out of reach. The dragon's scales felt smooth and surprisingly cool. All his heat must be on the inside.

Snarg knew what to do. Awkwardly, he lay down, avoiding the uncomfortable rocks and roots that broke through the forest floor.

Muncle gently eased the wing out from under the collar. As he did so, a single bright green scale fell to the ground. Muncle picked it up. It looked rather like a large leaf, but felt like a fingernail. He put it in his pocket. He was never likely to handle a dragon again, and he wanted a souvenir of this special moment.

Snarg opened the wing and flexed it. Muncle gasped. An unclipped dragon's wing was far bigger than he'd imagined. It was wider than Pa was tall.

"There you are, boy," he said. "Off you go now."

But Snarg didn't go anywhere. Instead he wriggled himself into a more comfortable position and began to lick his sore wing.

Muncle suddenly realized what was right before his eyes, and he couldn't believe his luck.

"Oh, thank you, Snarg!" he cried. "All I've got to do is take you home, and our troubles will be over! Gritt can go back to school. And Pa won't have to spend the Burps 'n' Farts prize money on a new dragon."

There was just one snag. How exactly was he going to *take* Snarg home?

The dragon couldn't squeeze through Muncle's secret gate. They would have to wait until after supper, when Pa unlocked one of the town gates to go hunting. Ma would be sick with worry by then, and he'd have to think up some excuse for being in the forest, but that couldn't be helped.

He settled down beside the dragon and started to think. How was he going to get Snarg to the town gate? Little was left of the long, heavy chain that Gritt would have used to lead him out onto the mountain.

"How did you manage that, Snarg?" Muncle said. "Was your breath so hot after hours in the sun that you just melted the rest away?"

Muncle could reach the last few links of the chain easily enough now, with Snarg lying down, but what would happen once the dragon stood up? He'd have no way of leading him to the gate, no way of controlling him at all. He could easily lose him all over again. Unless . . .

Muncle got up. He stepped lightly onto one of Snarg's front feet.

"Don't worry, Snarg," he said. "I don't weigh much. I won't hurt you. I might tickle a bit, though."

But Snarg didn't scratch or flick him off. Perhaps scales weren't as ticklish as skin. Climbing Snarg's leg was a bit trickier, but Muncle had practiced climbing tree trunks at his secret den, and his skills were coming in useful. Still the dragon went on licking. Muncle climbed higher, and was within reach of Snarg's collar, when the dragon suddenly swung his long neck around, and they came face to face. . . .

Snarg's fiery eyes, wide-open in surprise, dazzled Muncle, and the dragon's smoky breath blew into his

mouth and nose. He coughed and lost his grip, slithering toward the ground.

I'm going to break my legs, was his first thought.

I won't be able to sit for the Gigantia exam, was his second.

Or be in the Burps 'n' Farts competition, was his third.

Then, suddenly, Snarg's nose was under Muncle's bottom. He stopped sliding and found himself nudged back up. Grabbing the dragon's collar, he swung himself onto his back.

He'd done a good deed for Snarg, and now Snarg had done one for him. Gently, he patted the dragon's neck. Then he realized that being gentle was no good on scales, and instead gave him his hardest smack.

Snarg gave a snort of pleasure and settled down for a thorough wash. Muncle leaned over and watched as the purple tongue snaked around each scale of his front left foot. A little puddle of steaming dragon dribble was forming on the ground. Snarg worked his way up to his back, but he couldn't get to the bit that Muncle was sitting on, and ended up washing Muncle instead.

"*Ow!* Careful, Snarg," he yelped. "You're too hot."

Fortunately Snarg didn't care for the taste of grubby toes.

"*Ptherr*," the dragon coughed, and sent an arc of spittle flying between the trees.

Then he lumbered to his feet. He'd had enough of washing.

Muncle clung on, thrown forward and then backward.

"Snarg!" he gasped. "Are you really going to let me ride you? Is Mr. Thwackum wrong when he says it can't be done?"

And then he realized just what this could mean. They might not have to wait for Pa at all. The town gates weren't the only way into Mount Grumble. Not if you could ride a dragon with unclipped wings!

"Up, boy!" he ordered. "Up! Fly!"

Snarg plodded downhill through the trees.

Muncle pulled on his collar. He shouted. He pointed up.

Snarg broke into a trot. He wasn't getting the message at all.

"Oh, stupid me," Muncle said, wishing he'd gone to

more Dragon Science classes. "I'm doing it all wrong."

Holding on to the collar with one hand, he rummaged in his schoolbag with the other and found his dragon flute. It was only cheap pottery, but it had the same egg shape and three finger holes as Mr. Thwackum's silver one. He'd never used it on a real dragon, but he did know all the command signals. Now was the time to try them out.

He put the flute to his lips and blew three short blasts on the lowest note.

Snarg stopped.

"Well done, boy!"

It worked. He could do it!

"Now try this."

He blew again.

Forward! Turn right! Stop! Lie down!

Snarg obeyed them all.

Perfect. And now . . .

Up.

Snarg stood.

"No, Snarg," said Muncle. "Up again. *More* up. Fly! Fly to the sun!"

But the dragon just stood still. There *were* no signals

for flying. The flute was useless. They were going to have to wait for Pa after all.

Disappointed, Muncle turned Snarg toward the main gates, practicing his signals as they went. Changing direction when told, the dragon trudged steadily through the forest, weaving his way between trees and ducking under low branches, until they came to a clearing.

All at once Snarg broke into a trot . . . a canter . . . an ungainly gallop.

Muncle could feel his lunch of acorn bread roll and muddy water sloshing up and down inside him. The dragon was now moving as fast as a Smalling cart. It was just as terrifying. More terrifying, in fact, because Muncle was too far from the ground to jump off.

"Slow down!" he screamed. "Careful! Not so fast! Mind the trees!"

But there were no signals for any of these instructions, either. Hurriedly he stuffed his flute in his pocket so he could hang on to Snarg's collar with both hands.

He was only just in time. As they came to the widest part of the clearing, Snarg at last had room to spread both wings. He flapped them rapidly, sending gusts of wind swirling around Muncle's head. A massive oak tree loomed in front of them. Muncle shut his eyes and waited for the crash.

But it didn't come.

He opened his eyes again to see the oak tree falling away below them.

They were flying!

EIGHT

"Aaah!" gasped Muncle. His lunch wasn't sloshing anymore. His whole stomach had been snatched out of him. He looked down, fully expecting to see his insides tumbling to earth, but there was nothing below him now. No insides, no trees, just cloud.

"No!" Muncle cried. His sweaty hands slipped on the iron collar and shook so much he was afraid they would let go without him meaning them to. "No, Snarg! I've changed my mind. Let's go back. Let's wait for Pa after all. *Please.* PLEASE!"

But Snarg climbed higher. Farther from the ground. Farther from Muncle's insides.

This was definitely worse than being upside-downed by Gritt. He clamped his eyes tightly shut, but sensed his surroundings getting brighter. Then the thick, damp air was gone and he was surrounded by warmth. It was like being in the depths of the Dragon Farm, but without the smell.

Snarg stopped flapping his wings.

"No, Snarg," Muncle gasped. "No! You can't stop flying now! We'll crash!"

But they didn't. Snarg floated in lazy circles with just the occasional flap of his wings. Muncle's stomach settled back into place. He stopped feeling sick. He stopped clutching Snarg's collar quite so tightly. Finally he dared to open his eyes—but had to shut them again straight away. The sun was blindingly bright up here, brighter even than in the Smalling town. He opened and closed his eyes at least a hundred times before he got used to it. Then he looked down at the dazzling white carpet below them. It stretched as far as he could see in every direction. If someone had told him about this he wouldn't have believed them, wouldn't have believed that anywhere could stretch so far or be so white.

"Where are we, Snarg?" he breathed. "Is that what snow looks like? Is there snow on Mount Grumble?"

The white carpet was thick in some places and thin in others. As he watched, a hole suddenly appeared—and through it he could see what looked like rows of dragon scales far below. Then he realized what they were—Smalling roofs! They were right above the Smalling town! The carpet wasn't snow at all. It was what cloud looked like from above.

"No!" Muncle was horrified. One of the few things he had learned in Dragon Science was that dragons were extinct in the wild and all the ones in captivity belonged to giants. It was as important to hide their guard-dragons from the Smallings as to keep out of sight themselves.

Forgetting his fear of flying, he took one hand off Snarg's collar and reached for his flute. Urgently he blew the signals for "sit down" and "lie down." Snarg did the nearest thing he could in midair: He dived into the cloud.

Muncle lost his stomach again. He prayed they weren't heading toward the Smalling town.

Then ground broke through the fluffy white carpet—bare, rocky ground. . . .

"The Crater!" Muncle whooped. "We're back in Mount Grumble! Well done, boy. You couldn't have done better if I'd known a signal for 'go home.'"

They came in to land over the head of the Town Crier, who was delivering the evening news bulletin from his platform in the marketplace. He looked up as their shadow fell across him.

"Late extra!" he boomed, his voice rising with excitement. "Dragon Makes Off With Terrified Toddler!"

Snarg landed surprisingly lightly, hind legs first, and Muncle hardly bounced at all.

"No, no!" he yelled. "I'm not a toddler and I'm not terrified!"

And he wasn't. Not anymore. He was even sorry his dragon flight had come to an end.

"And he's not making off with me," he added. "He's coming home. He's the school dragon that escaped from the sunning station yesterday. I've just caught him."

"Correction!" announced the Town Crier. "Escaped Dragon Recaptured!"

There was no one to hear him. The shopkeepers and school children had gone home, and the grubhouses were now closed until the King's Birthday, to make sure they didn't run out of victuals on the great day.

Muncle blew his flute for "turn right" and steered the dragon to the school. Sitting high on Snarg's back meant that, for the first time in his life, he could reach the enormous iron door knocker. He heaved it up and let it drop against the door. *BANG!* It was so loud it made Muncle's ears throb.

"School's over for the day!" shouted the headmaster, Mr. Numskul, from somewhere inside. "I'm having my supper. Go away."

Muncle knocked again.

The door was wrenched open by an elderly giant with no hair and no chin.

"Are you deaf? I said g—"

When Mr. Numskul saw Snarg, his eyes goggled. Then he saw Muncle sitting on top of Snarg, and his mouth fell open to reveal a fine set of black stumps.

Muncle had never been able to look *down* on anyone

before. The fact that it was his headmaster he was look-ing down on made it even better. For a few moments he just sat there, grinning. Then he remembered his own supper. How long had he and Snarg been flying? Had Ma started to worry? He'd better get home. He slid reluc-tantly from Snarg's back.

"Your dragon, sir," he said. "The one my brother lost. That's Gritt Trogg. Gritt can come back to school now, can't he, sir?"

Mr. Numskul scratched his leathery head. "Well, yes," he muttered when he finally found his voice. "If the animal's not lost, the boy's not expelled."

Muncle felt bad about sending Snarg back to his stable now that he'd seen how a dragon was meant to live, flying free in the sunshine. But he had to do it. Gritt needed to go back to school if he was ever to become Chief Weapon-Maker.

"Bye, Snarg," said Muncle. He gave the dragon a friendly smack on the leg, and turned to go.

Snarg followed him.

"No!" cried Mr. Numskul. He yelled into the school. "Thwackum, come here at once. This is a job for you."

He seized a long claw-ended pole from the fearsome

tools that hung by the school door for dealing with unruly pupils. With it, he grabbed Snarg by the ear. The dragon let out a screech of pain.

"Not his ear!" cried Muncle. "You're hurting him. It's the one place he hasn't got scales."

"Do you think I don't know that, Trogg?" growled Mr. Numskul. "This is the only way to handle a rogue dragon."

"But he's not a rogue dragon," began Muncle. "He just needs—"

The headmaster wasn't listening. He hauled the screeching dragon back onto the doorstep. Snarg took one look at the oak door studded with iron nails, drew a deep breath in through his mouth, and let out a lungful of fiery sunshine through his nostrils.

The wooden door instantly burned to ash, and its red-hot nails and knocker clattered noisily to the ground. Mr. Thwackum's shocked face appeared through the cloud of smoke.

"Now look what you've done, Trogg!" roared Mr. Numskul, grabbing Muncle by the throat. He threw the pole to Mr. Thwackum, who began dragging the upset Snarg inside. "You're worse than your wretched brother.

We'll hear what your pa has to say about this. You come with me." Mr. Numskul's grip tightened.

Muncle could feel his air supply running out, and was just thinking that he wouldn't live to hear what Pa had to say, when the town gong rang out across the Crater.

Bong bong bong. Pause. *Bong.* Pause. *Bong bong bong.* Pause. *BONG.*

It was the fire alarm.

Mr. Numskul swung round.

Smoke was pouring from the school—and Snarg was peering out of a window triumphantly.

The headmaster let out a howl of fury and hurled Muncle to the ground. He raced back to the school as a terrified Mr. Thwackum dashed into the Crater, and the first of the firemen arrived, fire-beating brooms at the ready.

Muncle rubbed his throat back into its normal shape, gulped down several lungfuls of air, and got painfully to his feet.

He began to run. He had to get home and break the news to Pa before he heard it from the Town Crier.

Muncle was in giant-sized trouble.

NINE

The next morning, a small gong sounded in the street-tunnel outside the Troggs' home, followed by some muffled words. A messenger from the Town Crier's information service was on his way around the town with an important announcement.

"What's that about the school fire?" snapped Pa, banging his porridge bowl down on the table. He'd been in a foul mood since Muncle had come home the night before with the news of Snarg's fire-raising. It hadn't helped that he'd accused Muncle of lying about dragon-riding, and then had to say sorry after the Town Crier had reported a rogue dragon flying in the Crater with a minikin on its back. "Why can't these chaps shout louder? Make yourself useful for once, Gritt, and open the door."

Gritt got up instantly and did as he was told. He'd seemed on edge since yesterday, and when he wasn't avoiding Pa, he was doing his best not to annoy him. Muncle wondered what he was up to.

"Gigantia exams to go ahead despite fire at school," cried the messenger. "All pupils taking the Gigantia to report to school immediately."

"There you are, Muncle," said Ma. "It can't have been anything like as bad as you said."

"Well, don't just sit there, lad!" roared Pa. "Get yourself to school at once!"

"But Mr. Numskul will never let me take the exams now, Pa." Any hope that he'd had of passing the Gigantia had gone up in smoke along with the school.

"You don't know that unless you go and find out. The messenger said *all* pupils."

Muncle picked up his schoolbag. He felt hopeless.

"You've had no breakfast again," said Ma. "Here, take a cold roast stoat to have with your roll.

That should keep you going. Good luck, Muncle."

"Yeah," said Gritt. "Good luck. And thanks for catching Snarg. It wasn't your fault he burned the school down."

"Thanks," said Muncle.

He ran all the way to school but was still the last to arrive. Mr. Numskul stood in the doorway, checking everyone in. He was wearing an interesting pattern of bandages.

"Ah, Muncle," he snarled. "Most troublesome of all the Troggs. I suppose you thought your little trick with the overheated dragon would get the exams canceled. Well, tough luck. Get along to the hall at once."

Muncle couldn't believe it. He was going to be allowed to take his exams! And with all he'd learned about Smallings and dragons yesterday, he wouldn't just pass, he'd pass *well*. No one had ever given a flying display on a dragon before. Today he was going to get the marks he deserved. By tonight he'd definitely have two exam medals.

He hurried through the smoky, sooty corridors to the school hall, where he found the rest of his class sitting in a huddle in the middle of the floor. The teachers sat in the corners, on chairs they must have brought in from home. Every piece of school furniture had been burned to a crisp.

Muncle was about to join his class on the floor when everyone else scrambled to their feet. Mr. Numskul climbed the steps to the hall's stone platform and began sending pupils to different examiners. He kept Muncle waiting till last.

"Muncle Trogg, Dragon Science."

Muncle looked around for Mr. Thwackum, but he was nowhere to be seen.

"In the stables, you stupid boy. Do you think we'd allow dragons in the hall?"

The school stables lay one level below the classrooms, down a winding flight of rocky steps. Mr. Thwackum was waiting in his office. He was wearing bandages, too, and looking very sour.

"You know the rules, Trogg," he said. "There are seven parts to the exam and you need to pass five of them to pass the whole exam. You may choose your dragon."

The long corridor in front of the office was lined on either side with stalls, each with an iron stable-door.

Normally the upper doors were kept open, but if a dragon was in an aggressive mood—throwing flames or biting his neighbor—they could be shut. Today one of the upper doors was closed. It was Snarg's. The door was a funny shape. It looked as though Snarg had tried to melt his way out. Muncle pointed to it.

"I'll have that one," he said.

"Oh, no," said Mr. Thwackum hurriedly. "It took four of us to get him into that stall last night, and the other two are still in the hospital. We're waiting for the King's Dragon Master to come and put him down."

"What?" gasped Muncle.

Snarg didn't deserve to die. And Muncle needed him. Snarg was the only dragon he'd practiced on. He didn't know if he could control any of the others.

A nasty smile slid across Mr. Thwackum's face.

"All right," he said, "have it your way. You can open up that stall, but you'll be on your own. I'll be in my office, watching you through the bars in the door."

The teacher backed away speedily.

Muncle walked up to the closed stable, watched from the other stalls by the flaming orange eyes of the other dragons.

"Snarg," he called, "you remember me, don't you?"

As soon as he spoke, he realized the danger. Snarg might well remember him, but *how*? As the boy who'd freed his trapped wing? Or the boy who'd led him back to his stable prison?

It was a risk he had to take. He went to the equipment cabinet and found a whip. Several of the other dragons snorted in alarm when they saw it, but Muncle merely used it to reach up and unlatch Snarg's upper door. When Snarg looked out, the first thing he saw was the whip, too. He immediately shot a jet of white-hot flame at it. The leather lash shriveled, leaving Muncle with just the iron handle.

"Told you so!" Mr. Thwackum shouted gleefully through the bars.

"It's all right, Snarg," Muncle said gently. "I only wanted the handle anyway. Look." He reached up with it again and unlatched the lower door.

"No!" cried Mr. Thwackum, but Snarg was already out of his stable and giving Muncle a welcoming nuzzle.

"Steady, boy," said Muncle. "Your nostrils are still quite hot, you know. Now, show Mr. Thwackum how well behaved you are. Sit!"

But Snarg had no intention of sitting. He head-butted Muncle, gently but firmly, as if trying to tell him something. Muncle reached into his bag for his dragon flute and blew the two notes that meant "sit."

Snarg lay down.

Mr. Thwackum chortled triumphantly.

"Sit!" Muncle hissed.

Snarg stretched out a front leg.

This time Muncle understood. Quickly he climbed from foot to knee to shoulder, and settled into his riding position behind Snarg's collar.

There was no sound from the office now.

"Good boy," Muncle said. "Now, sit, please." He blew the command on the flute again.

Snarg leaped to his feet and trotted briskly up the ramp toward the exercise yard.

"Oh, no, Snarg," Muncle said. He felt guilty. "I haven't come to set you free again!"

But Snarg just kept on going. As they came to the double doors at the top of the ramp, Mr. Thwackum found his voice.

"Stop!" he yelled, but it was too late.

"It's all right!" Muncle called. "I'll do my advanced

exercises first and the easy commands when we come back." He reached out with his whip handle and unlatched the doors. Snarg butted them open.

The exercise yard was separated from the rest of the Crater by high walls. It was a large area, meant for exercising several dragons at a time. There was more than enough room between the walls for Snarg to spread his wings. More than enough room for him to reach takeoff speed . . .

It was busy in the Crater. Builders were putting up grandstands for the King's Birthday, and the King's guards were practicing their marching. All work came to a stop when Snarg cleared the walls of the exercise yard and headed for the clouds. Plenty of people saw Muncle's dragon-riding skills—but not Mr. Thwackum, who was still out of sight in his office.

"No, Snarg, not yet," Muncle urged, blowing the "turn right" signal in the hope that it would make the dragon start circling. "Mr. Thwackum's got to see us."

Snarg *did* circle low over the Crater, but not for long. He must have practiced a lot of moves during his day of freedom, and when he got bored he started to show off.

Steep dives and turns. Then a series of rolls that made Muncle feel sick. Again.

"No, Snarg!" he gasped, hooking his arms through the dragon's collar so he wouldn't fall off. "We don't need to be this clever. No one else can fly at all. Just circling will do."

The dragon finished with a spectacular loop. By the time Muncle was upright again he was so dizzy he felt as if there was a swarm of wasps in his head.

Below him the people in the Crater cheered. He looked down, and saw that someone had finally appeared in the exercise yard. It was hard to recognize him, because he was clad from head to foot in armor. Mr. Thwackum was taking no chances.

"All right, Snarg." Muncle blew the "lie down" signal. "He's seen us. Just a good landing and he'll have to give me top marks."

But Snarg wasn't ready to land yet. He climbed up and up, until they were high above the clouds.

Muncle understood just how he felt. "Oh, Snarg," he said wistfully, "if only we could run away together, you and me. I could live in my den and hunt for food like Pa does, and you could have hours of sunshine every day.

But you've got to stay in Mount Grumble so Gritt won't be expelled. And if we don't go back, I'll miss my next exam. At least you'll be safe from the King's Dragon Master, now that Mr. Thwackum has seen you're not out of control."

He tried the signal for "lie down" again, and Snarg dived at once. Perhaps he was tired after all that showing off and *wanted* to lie down.

More cheers went up as they flew back into the Crater. At the sight of Snarg approaching, Mr. Thwackum fled inside as fast as his clanking armor would allow, and locked the double doors behind him.

He was not there to see the perfect landing.

Muncle lowered himself from Snarg's back and banged on the doors. They opened just enough for Mr. Thwackum to reach around with a pair of dragon shears in his hand.

"Here," he said, throwing them to Muncle. "Clip his wings."

Snarg let out an enraged snort, put down his head, and charged.

Mr. Thwackum squeaked, and slammed the doors.

"No!" cried Muncle, afraid Snarg would break his

neck, but at the last moment the dragon changed direction and took off. In next to no time he had disappeared into the clouds.

"It's safe now, sir!" Muncle shouted. "Snarg's gone."

Mr. Thwackum reached around the doors again. This time he grabbed Muncle by the scruff of the neck and carried him to his office. On his desk lay two marking sticks: a white stick for correct answers and a black stick for wrong ones. Dropping Muncle to the floor, he picked up his knife and the black stick.

"'Sit' command," he said, cutting a notch. "No marks. 'Stand,' no marks. 'Lie,' 'stop,' 'fetch,' 'chase'"—he cut five more marks, savagely—"NO MARKS. As for 'burn,' the less said the better!

"Muncle Trogg, you have *failed* Dragon Science."

TEN

"What?" said Muncle. "But I *rode* a dragon. I *flew* a dragon."

"Riding and flying aren't on the curriculum. Sit, stand, lie, stop, fetch, chase, burn: That's what's in the exam."

"But—"

"No buts." Mr. Thwackum thrust Muncle's well-notched black stick into his hand. Then, for good measure, he took the unblemished white one and snapped it in half.

It's not fair, Muncle thought as he plodded wretchedly

back up the stairs. *The first thing I've ever been good at in my life, and it doesn't count. It's not fair, it's not fair, it's not FAIR!*

Back up at classroom level, the corridor was full of children comparing their results so far. Titan had got so many notches that his white sticks were almost falling apart. Brutus had a black eye and one arm in a sling as a result of being paired with Titan in the Martial Arts exam. Colossa and Valkyrie were arguing over who had produced the bigger piece of copper in Mining. Muncle saw them only mistily through his tears of disappointment. He ducked into one of the burned-out classrooms and sat down in a sooty corner out of sight of all those white sticks.

I should have run away with Snarg, he thought. *Even if I had to eat dried leaves and beetles, it would be better than staying at home with no chance of a job and Pa angry all the time.* But it was too late now. Snarg was gone. He would never see him again. And he wasn't brave enough to run away on his own.

The lunch gong sounded. Muncle wasn't hungry, but he'd had no breakfast, and he needed to keep his strength up for this afternoon's Smalling Studies exam.

As he forced down a few mouthfuls of stoat and roll, he ran through everything he knew about Smallings. It was a lot.

I'll still be taking home one exam medal, he told himself. *I won't let Ma and Pa down completely.*

The gong sounded for the end of lunch. Back in the hall, some of the afternoon exams had already started. The noise was deafening and the temperature rising. The screams of the children who weren't doing too well at Martial Arts rang out above the clank of hammer on anvil as children doing Metalwork put the finishing touches to spoons and spears. In the Mining corner, a furnace burned as fiercely as an overheated dragon while sweating students struggled to extract copper and iron from the ores they'd been digging up all term.

"Muncle Trogg!" yelled Mr. Numskul, above the din. "Where is . . . Ah, there you are. Muncle Trogg—Smalling Studies."

When he got to Miss Bumfit's corner of the hall, Muncle was surprised to find she was not alone. Biblos was there, too.

"The Wise Man is responsible for education in Mount Grumble," Miss Bumfit explained with her usual scowl.

"He checks some of our exams to make sure high standards are maintained. Remember to treat him with the Utmost Respect."

Muncle immediately felt better. Biblos was the only person outside his family who'd ever been kind to him. With Biblos asking the questions, Muncle just knew he could do well.

But Biblos was having trouble with his ear trumpet in the noisy hall and it was Miss Bumfit who started the exam.

"First question," she said, brandishing a black stick. "The Law With Regard to Smallings. Recite it, please."

That was easy. You didn't even have to go to school to know the Law. Everyone knew it. The giants had lived by its rules for hundreds of years. He chanted:

"Smallings are evil, Smallings are mean,
Smallings would kill our King and our Queen
If ever a giant or dragon was seen.
Keep in the cloud, keep to the night,
Keep in the mine, keep out of sight.
If Smallings should ever discover our town
They'd hunt every single man, wife, and child down."

"Excellent," said Biblos. He put his ear trumpet down for a moment while he cut a notch in the white stick. "It's Muncle, isn't it?" he went on, as if he had only a hazy memory of him. "The one who tried on the Smalling clothes at the museum? Describe those clothes for us, please."

Dear, clever Biblos. This was going to be easy, too. Muncle quickly rattled off a detailed description of the clothes.

"And they're soft," he ended. "Very soft. I can move easily in them."

"You *can* move easily in them?" said Miss Bumfit. "What do you mean, you *can*?"

"Could," said Muncle quickly. "I *could* move easily in them, when I tried them on. They're not stiff, like string cloth."

Biblos made another notch in his white stick.

"He doesn't get a mark for that," snapped Miss Bumfit. "It was too easy. Of course he can remember clothes he's actually worn."

"All right. The next right answer won't count," Biblos said reluctantly. "Tell us about the Book, Muncle."

"Briefly this time," added Miss Bumfit.

Muncle wasn't brief at all. He could still remember the symbols he'd practiced writing on his bedroom floor, and he wrote them again now for the examiners:

T R E A C L E T A R T

"So what does it mean?" demanded Miss Bumfit.

"I don't know," said Muncle, and then, realizing that it sounded as if he couldn't answer the question, he added, "I mean, *nobody* knows, not even the Wise Man. We just know that the symbols tell you how to do magic."

"Very good," said Biblos, but he didn't cut a notch. That was the answer that didn't count.

"Not good *enough*," said Miss Bumfit. "You need to tell us what magic *is*."

Muncle wasn't prepared for this one. He glanced at Biblos, who looked as if he wasn't prepared for it, either. You couldn't see magic, which made it hard to describe. Muncle did his best.

"It's something that Smallings have and we don't," he said. "It helps them to do things that they ought not to be able to do, like kill people who are a lot bigger than they are."

"Excellent," said Biblos, with a broad, toothless smile. "I couldn't have put it better myself."

"Homeland Security next," said Miss Bumfit curtly. "What would you do if you saw a Smalling near the gates of Mount Grumble?"

Muncle suspected a trap.

"I'll never see anyone near the gates," he said carefully, "because I'm never going to get the sort of job that lets me go outside the town."

"You're never going to get a job at all, Muncle Trogg, but that's not the point. You have to know the theory. What would you do in *theory*?"

Muncle knew this, because Pa was tested on it every year.

"Run to the nearest guard post," he said, "and have the alarm gong sounded. Shut the women and children in with their guard-dragons. Then go to my emergency station in the Crater and await further orders from the King's Guard."

"Wrong," said Miss Bumfit, triumphantly cutting a notch on her black stick. "You'd be no use at defending the town. You'd just get in the way."

"*Correct.*" Biblos overruled her firmly. "Muncle was

asked for the *theory*, and that is what he gave us."

He cut two notches to cancel out the one Miss Bumfit had just made.

"One last question," he said. "I know you're never going to meet a Smalling, Muncle, but if you did, how would you recognize him?"

Miss Bumfit snorted. "Far too eas—" she began, but Muncle had already launched into his answer.

"First there's the shape," he said, shutting his eyes to remember the scene in the alley more clearly. "Upright, with short arms. Then there's the clothes. Breeches that cover their ankles, and skirts that show their knees. Funny boots that stop at the top of the foot. Smooth skin. Shiny hair."

He opened his eyes to find his examiners staring at him in confusion.

"Miss Bumfit—" Biblos began.

"Don't look at me," she interrupted, angrily cutting notches on her black stick. "*I* haven't taught him this nonsense. I can't think what's come over him. He described their clothes perfectly well a few minutes ago. And no one should know better than him what a Smalling looks like. A Smalling, Muncle Trogg, is a pathetic little minikin just like *you*."

Muncle looked helplessly at Biblos, but the old man just shook his head sadly and laid his white stick aside. Muncle had given his examiners the correct answers, only they didn't know it.

He had failed. Again.

ELEVEN

The King's Birthday was the only holiday of the year in Mount Grumble. On that day every giant went to the celebrations in the Crater—even hunters in a bad temper and children in disgrace.

Pa elbowed his way through the crowd. Gritt shuffled along behind him, looking nervous. *What is he so worried about?* Muncle wondered as he followed him. *Gritt* wasn't the one who had to perform in the Burps 'n' Farts Competition in front of all these people. *Gritt* wasn't the one in disgrace for getting the worst marks on the Gigantia exam that anyone could remember. It was Muncle who should be nervous—and he was. Ma, bringing up the rear with Flubb on her back, ruffled his hair comfortingly.

Everyone had dressed in their holiday best, except the Troggs, who only had one set of clothes each. The grandstands were already full, but seats there cost five copper nugglins. The Troggs would be sitting on the ground, where it was free. Most of the best spots there were taken, too, but Pa just shoved people aside.

"We need to sit near the stage," he said firmly when Mrs. Bashpot objected. "We're the main act."

"Pa!" hissed Muncle. "We're just *an* act, not the *main* act."

"Do you want a good seat or don't you? Now sit down and shut up."

"Keep my place, will you?" said Ma. "I'll be back in a minute."

She thrust her way through the crowd and came back a few moments later with treats from the sweets stall. Lizard Licks for Gritt and Earthworm Chews for Muncle. Flubb, on Ma's back, was already digging into her Cobweb Candyfloss and covering Ma's hair with sticky threads.

Muncle didn't feel much like sweets just now but he knew Ma had saved up all year to buy them.

"Thanks," he said. "I'll keep them till after our play."

"Yeah, thanks," muttered Gritt. He shoved the Lizards into his pocket unlicked.

"Are you all right?" asked Ma.

"Of course I am," said Gritt, but his eyes darted around. "Why wouldn't I be?"

"You should think yourselves lucky!" said Pa. "You boys don't deserve treats this year."

"Oh, Pa, they're good boys, really," said Ma. "They've had a bit of bad luck, that's all."

"Bad *luck*?" Pa's voice rose. "To lose a dragon once might be bad luck, but to lose it twice *and* burn down the school . . ."

Everyone around them was starting to look.

". . . *and* fail the Gigantia . . ."

Gritt got to his feet in a hurry.

"I'm going to join my friends," he said, rubbing the three warts on his left ear nervously. "No one else is sitting with their parents."

"You won't get as good a seat as this," said Pa.

"Yes, I will. Thumper Plodd is saving me a place."

"Who?" said Ma.

Muncle shrugged. He wasn't going to spoil Ma's day by telling her that Thumper was Titan's second-in-command.

Gritt fought his way through the crowd nearly as forcefully as his parents, and soon disappeared from sight.

"Oh, well, all the more room for us," said Ma, settling her splendid bottom into Gritt's space. "Muncle isn't going to be able to see, Pa. Sit him on your shoulders."

"He's not a toddler. He can stand."

"I'm already standing," said Muncle, "and I can't see over Mrs. Bashpot's hairdo."

Mrs. Bashpot's hair was piled as high as a hedge, but it was nothing compared to Ma's. There were enough bramble branches braided into her hair to keep it standing on end for months. Ma's makeup was special, too. She had drawn black rings around her nostrils as well as her eyes. Even Flubb had been dressed up, her baby hair tied into a tuft with a ribbon of braided grasses.

"Go on, Pa," Ma said. "Let's forget our troubles for one day and just enjoy the King's Birthday."

Pa rolled his eyes but did as he was told, plonking

Muncle on his shoulders just as a rapid beating of the town gong announced the arrival of the Royal Family.

King Thortless, magnificent in fluffy sheepskin robes, strode to the front of the palace balcony overlooking the stage. His golden crown, studded with polished lumps of coal, sat on top of a pom-pommed sheepskin hat.

The crowd cheered and clapped, and King Thortless waved to them for several minutes before allowing the Queen and Crown Princess to join him.

Queen Fattipat was wearing a tall, narrow crown, with her hair poking out of the top of it like a crow's nest. Her lips were painted glossy black.

"I can't see!" protested a high-pitched, earsplitting voice from somewhere out of sight.

The crowd may not have been able to see Princess Puglug, but they could certainly hear her.

"Fetch a stool for her Royal Hugeness," ordered the King, and a few moments later the round face and pigtails of the Crown Princess appeared above the balcony rail. She waved madly at the crowd, and her copper tiara slipped over one eye.

Finally, Biblos shuffled to the front of the balcony and took his place beside the King.

The Steward of the King's Birthday stepped to the front of the stage.

"Congratulations to our beloved King Thortless the Thirteenth on the occasion of his thirty-third birthday," he declared. "Let the parade begin!"

With a crash of cymbals and drums, the King's Guard marched into the Crater, brandishing their bows and battle-axes. The craftsmen of Mount Grumble came next—weapon-makers waving their weapons, barrel-makers rolling their barrels—followed by some of Pa's hunter friends with dead animals slung over their shoulders. When the craftsmen and hunters had taken their seats, the King's Guard went up onto the stage and performed a very realistic mock battle.

"We should have weapons like that for our act!" muttered Pa.

"Sssh!" hissed Muncle, shuddering at the thought of adding deep cuts and broken bones to the bruises he was already expecting. "We don't want everyone to know about it yet."

Pa had a point, though. Muncle planned to hide a stick up his sleeve, but would people think it looked like a killing stick? He hoped their act really was going to be good enough.

The Dragon Division of the King's Guard went up on stage for the grand finale of the morning's entertainment. No one had ever managed to train a dragon to march in time to drums and cymbals, but the King's Dragon Master gave an impressive demonstration of dragon control. He made six dragons sit, stand, lie, stay, fetch, chase, and burn in unison.

The crowd roared with approval.

"Now let's see you riding and flying!" yelled Pa.

"Pa," groaned Muncle, blushing purple. "You're embarrassing me."

"Failing your Gigantia and burning the school down are embarrassing, lad." He patted Muncle's ankle awkwardly. "Riding and flying a dragon are things to be proud of." He sniffed. "It's just a pity they aren't *useful*."

Everything stopped while the Royal Family went into the palace for dinner. The grubhouse owners and innkeepers set up stalls laden with food and drink to sell to everyone else, and around the edge of the Crater, people crowded around the sideshow competitions—Biggest

Boil, Pussiest Pimple, Bash-the-Badger, Hedgehog Bowling.

Ma had brought a picnic: a bottle of sludge soup for Flubb, and cold owl pie and caterpillar crisps for the rest of the family. Pa happily ate Gritt's share as well as his own. When the gong sounded once more, everyone made their way back to their seats.

"Come on, Pa," said Muncle. "We've got to get to the dressing room under the stage."

"All right, all right." Pa jumped to his feet, slapping Muncle on the back. "This is where we turn our fortunes around. Fifty nuggets! You'd better not let the family down this time, Muncle."

There was barely enough height in the dressing room for most of the other competitors to stand upright, but Muncle had no problem. Turning his back on everyone else, he quickly changed into the Smalling clothes—which he'd kept safely in his bag—and wrapped his bedroom curtain around himself like a cloak to keep them hidden until the last moment. Pa had no grand sheepskin robes, but he had hollowed a crown out of a log.

"Here, give that to me, Pa," said Muncle. "I'll hide it under my cloak till you need it."

They climbed up onto the stage. While they'd been changing, benches had been put around the edge for the competitors, and two chairs were placed at the sides for the judges. The Steward of the King's Birthday sat in one, and Biblos came down from the palace balcony to sit in the other.

The Burps 'n' Farts Competition was about to begin!

TWELVE

One by one, the acts were called forward to perform. Pa and Muncle had to sit nervously through juggling, fire-eating, and knife-throwing, as well as a great deal of burping and farting, before it was their turn.

The Town Crier sounded his gong, softly at first but quickly rising to a deafening *CLANG!*

"And now," announced the Steward of the King's Birthday as the echo of the gong faded away, "Pa and Muncle Trogg with *Battle to the Death*!"

Muncle slipped the crown out from under his cloak.

Pa put it on and swaggered into the middle of the stage. Some people laughed. Others booed.

"Who does he think he is?" said a voice in the crowd. "Why is he making fun of the King?"

Muncle hurriedly followed Pa to the middle of the stage. He tripped over his curtain cloak and fell flat on his face. The crowd burst into laughter. This was not the start Muncle had hoped for. He scrambled to his feet and tried to carry on as if nothing had happened.

"Are you King Ogmagog the Fourth?" he asked as loudly as he could.

The shape of the Crater meant that even little voices could be heard. This time nobody booed. It was not King Thortless. Ogmagog the Fourth had died centuries ago, in the early days of Smalling magic.

"I am," said Pa. "And who might *you* be, little boy?"

"I'm not a little boy," cried Muncle, throwing off his cloak to reveal the museum clothes. "I'm a full-grown . . . Smalling!"

The crowd gasped. Somewhere a woman screamed. Children burst into tears. Muncle didn't need to be a good actor. His size and his strange clothes were realistic enough.

"And what do you want with me?" said Pa, doing his best to look frightened.

"For years you giants have turned my people into slaves and suppers. This has got to stop. *I* am going to turn *you* into supper."

At this point Muncle allowed his stick to slip down his sleeve into his hand. He pointed it at Pa.

"Die, King Ogmagog the Fourth!" he cried. "Bang! Bang!"

"No!" shouted the audience as one, and King Ogmagog obliged them by not dying. He lunged at Muncle.

Muncle dodged out of the way.

The crowd held their breath.

Then Pa caught him.

He tossed him in the air. He bounced him on the ground. He rolled him across the stage.

The crowd cheered.

"Ow! You're hurting me!" Muncle cried—and he wasn't acting.

But Pa was enjoying himself now. Throwing Muncle to the ground, he seized his stick and snapped it in half.

The crowd went wild. The Smalling and his magic killing stick had been defeated!

Pa stood over Muncle with one foot on his chest.

"Can't breathe!" gasped Muncle, trying to look dead.

"Sorry!" Pa picked up the curtain cloak and threw it over the body of the lifeless Smalling. Then he walked to the front of the stage and bowed long and low to the crowd—and longer and lower to the King.

The audience was still cheering when Muncle's breath came back. He crawled out from under the cloak. The first person he saw was Biblos, leaning forward in his chair, waving his ear trumpet and whooping as loudly as a man half his age.

Take a bow, Biblos mouthed, pointing toward the front of the stage.

Muncle limped forward. The cheering grew louder and Pa lifted him high in the air for the King and the crowd to see.

I did it! he thought, and his bruised chest swelled with a feeling he'd never known. *They liked it! I'M A SUCCESS!*

Then it was over. The cheering turned into a hum of conversation. The other contestants gathered around and the King came down from the balcony to present the prize of fifty nuggets. There was no doubt about who had won.

Suddenly there was a disturbance in the crowd. The Steward of the King's Birthday stepped to the front of the stage.

"Make way down there," he shouted. "We haven't finished yet. There's one final act."

Muncle squeezed between the legs of the other competitors to see what was going on.

Up the steps to the stage came Gritt and Titan. Between them they were carrying the covered silver dish meant for the King's sheep.

"What's going on here?" King Thortless demanded. "Guards, seize these two boys. That dish is mine. They've stolen it."

"Not stolen, Your Enormity," said Titan, as he and Gritt lowered the dish to the floor. "Borrowed. It contains a small present from your humble servant, Titan Bulge."

He whipped the cover off the dish.

Muncle gasped.

"What's this?" said the King. "Wise Man, where are you? Come and tell me what this is."

Muncle could have told him. He'd seen the King's birthday present before—but she hadn't been bound and gagged then. She'd been on her way to school.

Lying on the dish was the girl with the golden foxtail. It was Emily.

Biblos shuffled over from his chair. He took one look at Emily and turned to the King. He'd gone very pale.

"I believe . . . Your Enormity," he stammered, "I believe . . . that this is a Smalling."

The gasp that went up from the crowd now was far louder than the one that had gone up when Muncle had thrown off his cloak. A real Smalling was much more exciting and original than a pretend one.

"Is it alive?" said the King, prodding his present with his toe.

"It's not an it," said Titan helpfully. "It's a she. I looked."

The King poked Emily again. Muncle could see the terror in her blue eyes as half a dozen giants peered down at her. He looked away. What the bloggus was going to happen to the poor girl now?

The King turned to Titan. "This is indeed a most unusual present," he said. "Undoubtedly the highlight of my Birthday. And you thought it up all by yourself, young man?"

Muncle glanced at Gritt. No wonder he'd been nervous all day. He looked more troubled than ever now, shifting from one foot to the other as if he couldn't decide whether to stay or run.

"All by myself, Your Enormity," Titan said proudly.

"Seize him!" ordered King Thortless, and two guards immediately clamped their fists round Titan's arms. "Now, boy, recite the Law With Regard to Smallings. Nice and loud, so everyone can hear you."

"Smallings are evil," Titan muttered, *"Smallings are mean, Smallings would kill our King and—"*

"Stop there!" roared the King. "So you *do* know the Law. And you thought it was a good idea to bring me a present that would kill me?"

"She's just a tiny girl," Titan protested. "She couldn't kill anything."

Out of the corner of his eye, Muncle saw Gritt edging away. Now he didn't just look nervous—he looked terrified.

"Any Smalling can kill with a magic stick," snapped the King. "What have you done with hers?"

The whole Crater waited breathlessly for the reply.

"Ask Gritt Trogg," said Titan sullenly. "He kidnapped her, not me."

With stomach-churning certainty Muncle knew that Titan wasn't lying. Gritt *had* done it—but how? *He* couldn't fit through Muncle's broken gate—if he even knew where it was. He must have helped himself to Pa's key for the town gates. Pa always took it out of his pocket when he came home because it was uncomfortable to sleep on. And Gritt knew Pa's description of the way to the Smalling town as well as Muncle did. He must have waited at the edge of the town and grabbed the first Smalling who came along. He was just lucky it hadn't been one with a killing stick.

But his luck had run out now.

There were shouts near the edge of the stage as Gritt was found, trying to hide behind his father.

"There must be some mistake," protested Pa. "My boy wouldn't . . ."

The guards brushed him aside and seized Gritt.

"It wasn't my idea," he protested. "It was the Thunder Thugs. They said you had to do something against the law to—"

"To the dungeons with the pair of them," said the King.

"Gritt!" cried Ma, fighting her way onto the stage, her hairstyle collapsing and her face purple with worry as the guards dragged Gritt away. Flubb, happily innocent of all that was happening, busily tried to tidy her hair.

The King ignored Ma. "And tell my cook to take that sheep off the spit and put this Smalling on instead," he ordered. "There's no point in wasting her now that she's here."

THIRTEEN

"No!" cried Muncle.

"NO!" His plea was drowned out by a louder one from the palace balcony.

Footsteps thundered down stairs, and Princess Puglug burst onto the stage.

"I want her alive, Pa!" she cried. "She's cute. And you promised me another pet."

"So I did, Pugly dear." The King smiled fondly at his lovely daughter, who, at six years old, was as dainty as a dumpling. "There's not much meat on her anyway. She's all yours."

"Mmm!" protested the pet in the King's dish, thrashing around as best she could with her wrists and ankles tied together. "Mmmmm!"

Muncle ran across and snatched the gag from her face.

Emily stared up at him. "You're real, aren't you?" she croaked—she'd clearly been doing a lot of screaming and shouting. "You're not from the circus. You're real, live giants."

"Shh," hissed Muncle. "Don't tell them we've met before."

"But—"

"*Ssshhh!* If you tell them, they'll roast us both. . . ."

Princess Puglug tipped Muncle over with a swift kick.

"Out of my way, minikin," she said. "The Smalling's mine."

She knelt down and ripped the rope from Emily's hands and feet.

Muncle had never seen the Princess up close before. She was too royal to go to school. But watching her now, he could see that the games she wanted to play with Emily would be every bit as rough as the games Gritt played with *him*. He had to rescue her!

He pushed his way to the King's side.

"Your Enormity," he said, as loudly and as firmly as he could. "You can't keep her."

"Muncle!" hissed Ma and Pa together.

"How dare you tell My Enormity what to do?" said the King.

"*Please*, sire, I'm not being disrespectful. Biblos will explain what I mean."

"I will?" said Biblos.

"Of course," said Muncle. "It's the very reason kidnapping's against the law."

"Ah, yes. Well, you explain, Muncle." Biblos turned to the King. "Young Trogg here is quite an expert on Smallings," he said. "I think it would be fair to say he knows more about them than I do."

Muncle blushed purple again. Biblos must have guessed that he'd broken the Law to know as much as he did about Smallings, but he didn't give him away.

"Really? If you say so, Biblos . . . Well, out with it, minikin. Why can't we keep her?"

"Because they'll be looking for her, of course."

"They won't miss her," the King said airily. "She's too small to matter."

"Wouldn't you miss Princess Puglug, Your Enormity, if she disappeared?"

King Thortless turned on Muncle in fury. "How dare you compare this ugly little thing to my beautiful Puglug?"

"They *will* miss me!" Emily had found her voice and her courage. "They'll find you, you know. They'll flatten the forest and break down your gates and blow up the mountain! Ouch!"

Princess Puglug was combing Emily's yellow fox-tail with her ragged fingernails. "Smallings can't flatten trees," she said. "They're not big enough."

"I'm afraid they probably can," said the King, putting a protective arm around his daughter. "I wasn't going to tell you this until you were older, but the truth is, dearest, they can do more than you think. You see, Smallings have got magic."

Puglug gasped.

And Emily laughed. She actually laughed. *At the King.*

King Thortless seized Emily and shook her.

"How dare you laugh at My Enormity?" he growled.

"I didn't," said Emily. "I laughed at the idea that we use magic. There's no such thing."

"Don't lie to me, Smalling. We know you've got magic. My hunters have seen your carts that go without horses. My ancestors were killed by your ancestors' killing sticks. And just you tell me how you would flatten our gates and blow up this mountain without magic."

"With tanks and bombs," said Emily. "But it's not as if this mountain would need much help to blow up. It's done it before, all by itself, and it could do it again any time. That's why we have scientists to study it. In case we need to run away."

This time it was the giants who laughed.

"Mountains that blow themselves up?" chuckled the King. "Well, you tell a good fairy tale, I'll grant you that. You really will entertain my daughter. Here, minikin"—he tossed Emily to Muncle, who tried to catch her but was almost flattened in the attempt—"your hands are small enough to fit in her pockets. Empty them. I can't give her to Puglug till I'm sure she doesn't have any magic . . . er . . . thingies."

"It's not a fairy tale," protested Emily, as Muncle picked himself up and searched her pockets apologetically. "Last time it happened, it killed a lot of people. It buried our town, although it was only a village then. That's what made this great hole in the top of your mountain. Don't you realize it's a volcano?"

"Volcano?" said the King. "Ever heard of that, Biblos?"

"Volcano? Volcano?" The old man shook his head. "That's not a proper word. She's made it up. A trick to frighten us."

"All right," said Emily. "Don't believe me. But one day this mountain will burst open, and flames and melted rock will gush out of it, and you'll all be cooked alive inside. You must have noticed that smoke trickles out of it, and that it sometimes rumbles."

"Of course smoke trickles out of it," said the King. "We have fires and torches. And the rumbles are thunder." He leaned over Emily. "*Thun-der*—surely you've heard of that, you stupid Smalling?" He turned to Muncle. "Well, minikin, what have you found in her pockets?"

"Just this bit of paper." Muncle held up a crumpled white square.

"What's that for?" demanded the King.

"Blowing your nose on," said Emily, and she took the paper out of Muncle's hand and snorted into it.

Biblos shook his head in bewilderment. "I've been wrong all along," he muttered. "I always thought Smallings *wrote* on paper."

The King seemed satisfied. "She's all yours, Puglug my precious," he said, plonking Emily into his daughter's arms. "Let's go and show your new pet to your ma, then we'll all have birthday tea."

He led his daughter toward the palace doors with Emily struggling in her arms.

Muncle ran after them.

"Get me out of here!" Emily cried.

"I will, I will, just . . ."

"What is she saying, Pa?" asked Puglug. "I can't understand her funny squeaky voice."

"I'm finding it hard myself, precious one."

Muncle saw his chance. "*I* can understand her," he said. "Why don't I help the Princess?"

"Excellent idea," said Biblos. "Why didn't I think of that myself? I think you should let Muncle do that, Your Enormity." He dropped his voice. "She might

130

trust someone his size and give away Smalling secrets."

"Aha!" King Thortless whispered back. "Good plan, Wise Man."

And with that, he tucked Muncle under his arm, and carried him into the palace.

FOURTEEN

It was the first time Muncle had ever been inside the palace. But from under the King's arm he could see little more than the floor. The King stomped through room after room, and up a flight of stairs, before he stopped and dumped Muncle on the floor.

"You stay here," Puglug told him, "while I have birthday tea and show Ugly Thing to Ma. We'll be back later."

Emily waved frantically at Muncle as she was carried back out of the room, and he smiled and nodded, which he hoped she would understand meant, *Don't worry, it's all right, I'm going to get you out of here.*

But Muncle had no idea how to sneak out of a massive palace guarded by extra-strong giants with battle-axes.

The door banged shut behind Puglug and the King, and the key rattled in the lock. It wasn't just the outer palace doors that Muncle had to worry about. He couldn't even get out of this room.

He seemed to be in Puglug's bedroom, which was bigger than the Troggs' whole home! A fire burned in an iron grate and the smoke disappeared through a hole in the ceiling instead of filling the room. On a table, beside three lighted candles, was a dead hedgehog for brushing the Princess's hair, and a pot of furry green gravy to make her smell nice.

And there were more toys than Muncle could count. (He'd had two toys in his whole life—a wooden rattle, made by Pa, which now belonged to Flubb, and a wooden sword, also made by Pa, which Gritt used as a dagger.) Dolls were scattered everywhere, and there were dolls' chairs, a dolls' table, dolls' bowls and mugs, a dolls' clothes chest, and even a dolls' box bed with a doll tucked up in it.

He was just trying out a dolls' chair for size when a sudden *kerflump* made him jump. He leaped up, thinking someone had opened the door. But there was no one there. Then he heard the faintest of footsteps behind him. He spun around.

"Blistering bogspots!" he gasped.

Padding softly across the floor came a baby Rainbow Royal. It curled up in a sheepskin-lined basket by the fire. Muncle couldn't believe it. A few giants, like Titan's pa, liked to walk their guard-dragons around the town to show how tough they were, but even they wouldn't have given one to a child as a pet. He knelt down beside the basket.

He could tell at once that the animal wasn't very well. Its eyes looked more like dying embers than blazing flames, and when he reached a hand out to stroke it, he found the dragon's nostrils were cool.

"They've been giving you water to keep you quiet, haven't they?" he said. He took one of the dragon's paws in his hands. "Oh, you poor thing," he said, wincing. "They've pulled your claws out, too."

Muncle looked around the room again. He began to think. . . .

There was no litter tray, and a dragon this young would not be housebroken. Either a servant took the Rainbow Royal down to the King's stables, or . . .

Excitedly Muncle jumped to his feet. He was sure the dragon hadn't been in the room when he'd first looked around. There had to be another way in—and out!

He ran across the room to where he thought the Royal had come from—a dark wall farthest from the fire and the candles. Muncle fumbled his way along it, feeling for a knob, a latch, or a catch. He had nearly reached the corner and was about to give up when the wall gave way. He fell through into total darkness.

A dragon flap!

He seemed to be in a narrow tunnel that wasn't even high enough for *him* to stand up in. It must lead to the royal stables, but he didn't dare explore it now. He had to be in Puglug's bedroom when she came back. He pushed his way back through the dragon flap to the Rainbow Royal.

"Thank you," he said, rubbing the dragon's nose between his hands to warm it up. "I think you may have shown me how to escape."

Footsteps sounded in the corridor outside and Puglug burst into the room, dangling Emily by one arm.

"Oh, you've found Draggly," the Princess said with

a yawn. "He's boring. He won't play. Ugly Thing's going to be much more fun. She hasn't taken her tea, though, naughty girl."

She dumped Emily on a dolls' chair.

Emily rubbed her shoulder. "Nasty brute!" she said tearfully. Her frightened blue eyes looked too big for her pale little face.

"What did she say?" demanded Puglug.

"Er . . . tasty fruit!" said Muncle. "I think she wants fruit."

Puglug took a chunk of birthday cake out of her pocket and licked the fluff off it. Then she put it on the table.

"We haven't got any fruit," she said, "so stop being fussy. If you don't eat up, I'll put you to bed hungry."

"I'd rather starve!" Emily hiccupped through her tears.

"What did she say?"

"I didn't quite catch it. I'll see if I can get her to speak up."

Muncle sat on the dolls' chair next to Emily's. "It's going to be all right," he whispered. "I've got a plan."

"Really?" Emily didn't sound sure.

"I'll tell you later, after the Princess has gone to bed. Just do what she wants. Eat your cake."

"*Cake?* That's supposed to be cake? It tastes as if it's made from worms and slugs and toadstools."

"Isn't that the sort of cake you like?" he asked, surprised.

"Are you crazy?"

"Well, just pretend to eat it and then slip it to me under the table."

Bit by tiny bit the cake disappeared.

"That's better," said Puglug. "Bedtime now."

She picked Emily up and started to pull off her clothes. Muncle was astonished. Did royalty take their clothes off to go to bed? Embarrassed, he turned his head away, but glanced out of the corner of his eye. Were Smallings' bodies as free from warts and bristles as their faces? Emily put up a brave struggle but eventually her shirt and skirt came off. Then Muncle got a real shock. She was wearing more clothes underneath!

Puglug seemed surprised, too, but threw a doll out of its bed and shoved Emily between the sheepskin blankets just as she was.

Then she turned her attention to Muncle.

"Now, minikin," she said, "where can I put *you* to bed?"

"No!" said Muncle, alarmed at the idea of losing *his* clothes. "No, I'm not going to bed."

"You know what happens to little boys who won't go to bed, don't you?" said the Princess. "I shall have to give you a sound spanking."

Before Muncle could protest, she tipped him face down over her knee and walloped his bottom.

"Ouch!" he cried, which delighted Puglug so much that she promptly walloped him again. This time he had the sense to clench his teeth and make no sound. "Please be careful, Your Hugeness," he managed to say. "These Smalling breeches are your father's property. You have to treat them with the Utmost Resp—Ouch!"

"They'll be MY property one day, so I can do what I like with them!" cried Puglug, yanking off his boots and socks.

"No!" cried Muncle again, but before the Princess could start on his breeches, the bedroom door opened and in shuffled an old woman wearing a string-cloth apron and cap.

"Bedtime, Your Hugeness," the woman announced, blowing out two of the candles.

"Not yet, Nursie," protested Puglug. "Pa said I could stay up late 'cause it's his birthday."

"That's not what His Enormity told *me*." The nurse turned back the top two sheepskin blankets in Puglug's box bed, and smoothed out the bottom ones. "And you know what happens to little princesses who won't go to bed, don't you?"

"Oh, all *right*. But I have to find somewhere for minikin to sleep." Puglug's eye lit on Draggly's basket.

"This'll do," she said, and plonked Muncle down beside the baby dragon. "Night-night, Draggly." The Princess kissed the dragon twice on the nose. "Night-night, minikin . . ."

Too late, Muncle realized what was coming next.

Puglug's face loomed above him. She bent closer . . . and closer . . . and closer . . .

Yeeugh! Slimy slobber crawled down Muncle's cheek.

Hurriedly he pulled one of Draggly's wings across his face, and the second kiss landed harmlessly on the dragon's rainbow scales.

It was warm next to the dying fire. The sheepskin

blanket was softer than anything Muncle had ever felt before. It had been a long, exciting day, and he was very tired, but he forced himself to stay awake while Puglug's nurse dressed the Crown Princess for bed in a splendid knitted nightie decorated with bats' wings.

Before long the room started to vibrate to Puglug's snores, and the old nurse settled in a chair with her bone knitting needles and a huge ball of string.

Clatter-atter-atter . . .

Muncle woke with a start as a knitting needle fell, rattling on the stone floor. Nursie, her head back and her mouth open, was snoring even louder than Puglug. How long had he been asleep? Quite a while, judging by the last candle burning on the dressing table, which was now no more than a stump.

He scrambled out of the dragon basket.

He had to rescue Emily quickly—while there was still time.

FIFTEEN

Muncle tiptoed to the table and took the candle stump. Then he crept to the dolls' bed.

"Emily." He whispered her name so softly, he was afraid she might not hear him above the din of snoring. "Are you awake?"

"Of course I'm awake," she sobbed. "How could anyone sleep in this horrible place?"

Horrible? Muncle couldn't imagine a more magnificent room, but this was not the time to argue.

"Come on, then," he whispered. "I know a way out."

"How do I know you aren't taking me somewhere even worse?"

"What *could* be worse? If you stay here, Puglug will play with you until she gets bored, and then her pa will eat you."

There was only a short pause before Emily sniffed. "All right." She sat up, holding a sheepskin around her.

"Can you see my clothes anywhere?" she whispered.

"They're here, on the floor." Muncle handed them over.

"Don't look while I get dressed. . . ."

Muncle turned his back and waited.

"All right. You can turn around now."

They looked at each other by the light of the candle. Emily was about as tall as Flubb, but much, much thinner. Muncle felt as if he was the big brother and she was the little sister he had to protect. "I don't even know your name," she whispered.

"Muncle."

"Michael?"

"Muncle. Come on—"

"*Shnaaargh!*" Puglug turned over with an extra-loud snore.

Emily jumped. "It's all right," Muncle whispered. "They're both still asleep. And here's the way out— look!"

By candlelight it was easy to see the dragon flap in the wall. Muncle held it open for Emily. She could stand upright inside.

"You're safe now," said Muncle. "No giant can get to you in here."

"Except you. How old are you?"

"Ten."

"Really? Same as me! Then why are you so small?"

"I don't know. *No* one seems to know. Come on, follow me."

Bending his knees and bowing his head, Muncle edged along the tunnel sideways. It was awkward, but that way his body didn't screen the candlelight from Emily.

"Where does this passage go?" she asked, as they shuffled downhill around bend after bend.

"The stables. We'll be able to get out without going past the guards."

That, at least, was what Muncle hoped.

"Stables? You keep horses inside your mountain?"

"Er . . . not horses, exactly." He stopped abruptly. "Oh, *no.*"

In front of them the passage split into two.

"One way must lead to the stables . . ."

"You mean you don't *know* which?"

Trying to look confident, Muncle set off down the left-hand tunnel. "Let's try this one," he said. "We can always come back if it's wrong."

They hadn't gone much farther before the tunnel widened out and Muncle found he, too, could stand upright. He raised the candle above his head and looked around. They were surrounded by barrels. Phew, it was really warm this far into the mountain! It reminded Muncle of the Dragon Farm, but there were no dragons here, so why was it so hot?

"This doesn't look like stables," said Emily.

"It's not," said Muncle excitedly. He forgot about the heat. "It's better than the stables. This is the King's ale-warming cellar. And I know the way out."

He'd often seen Dripso Drooling, the innkeeper from the Slurp and Slobber, delivering the King's ale—and it went down a trapdoor in the Crater, just in front of the palace kitchens. And there was the trapdoor! It was far

above their heads, but there was a ramp leading up to it—the King had ordered his beer to be rolled rather than dropped, in case the barrels burst open and spilt his precious ale.

But the ramp was steep. They crawled up it . . . and slipped back. Up and back. Up and back. Emily quickly got very tired and red in the face.

"Here," said Muncle, wriggling down behind her. "I'll push you."

That was better. Soon they were kneeling at the top of the ramp, just under the hefty bolt that stopped anyone opening the trapdoor from the outside and stealing the King's ale. Muncle studied it. It was heavy, but as it was used often, it was well-greased and free from rust.

"You pull on the handle," he said, "and I'll push the bolt."

He put down the candle stump so he could use both hands. It tipped over, rolled down the ramp, and went out. They were plunged into total darkness.

"Oh, no!" squealed Emily. "I can hardly breathe it's so hot in here, and now I can't see, either."

"It's all right, Emily. I've still got my hand on the

bolt. We'll be outside in a moment, then there'll be fresh air and moonlight."

The bolt shot open surprisingly easily. But the door didn't drop down.

"It must open outward," said Emily in the darkness. She sounded frightened now. "We're never going to be strong enough to push it up."

Freedom was the other side of just one door, but that door was as thick as Muncle's arm.

Muncle knelt at the very top of the ramp, his shoulders pressed against the trapdoor. With a huge effort he pushed himself to his feet, and the door creaked open a little way.

"Can you get through that gap?" he gasped. "Quick! I can't stand like this for very long."

Emily squeezed through.

"But what about you?" she said.

"Find something long and strong to lever the door up with," he gasped again. "There must be loads of rubbish lying around out there after the King's Birthday."

"But I'm not out anywhere," said Emily. "I'm just in another dark room. We haven't escaped at all."

SIXTEEN

"What?" Muncle was so surprised that he jerked up, taking the trapdoor with him. He scrambled out into the darkness, and jumped clear as the door slammed shut.

Then he took a few steps . . . and tripped over something. He picked it up, felt it all over, and whooped with delight.

"My bag!" he cried. "This is where I got changed. We *have* got out of the palace. It's just that we're under the stage. The way into the Crater is over here."

"The Crater?" said Emily as Muncle led her to a

doorway at the side of the stage. "So you *do* know it's a volcano."

"What do you mean?"

"A crater is the hole left behind when a volcano explodes."

Muncle felt the hairs all over his body stand on end.

"No," he said uncertainly. "It must be a word that's different in Smalling-speak. 'Crater' just means an open-air space."

"But—" Emily began. Then she stopped. "Is that really what you think?"

The thought Muncle had brushed aside in the ale-warming cellar came back to him. The giants' homes, the Crater, and the street-tunnels were always comfortably warm—but deep inside the mountain was much hotter. Could Emily possibly be right? He didn't have time to think about it now. Getting her home was much more important.

He peered out of the stage doorway. The Crater was deserted.

"Come on."

"What about the guards?"

"In their sentry boxes outside the front door. They can't see us from there."

Emily and Muncle tiptoed out from under the stage. The center of the Crater was moonlit, but the balconies of the palace and other grand houses created deep shadows at the edges. Holding hands, the two of them ran through the shadows until Muncle dove off without warning down a side street-tunnel.

Emily stumbled and fell.

"You're going too fast for me," she said, gasping. "I've got a stitch in my side."

"We have to get out of the Crater quickly," Muncle whispered anxiously.

"But I don't like these dark tunnels. I wish we still had the candle."

"We put our torches out at night," Muncle explained. "But don't worry. I know this tunnel like the warts on my thumb."

He wouldn't be happy until they were out of Mount Grumble and in the forest.

"I'll carry you," he said, and before she could protest, he hoisted her onto his back. Then, keeping one hand against the street-tunnel wall to guide him, he half walked, half ran to his broken gate, where he put her down again.

He breathed a sigh of relief as he squeezed through, then held back the ivy and brambles for Emily to follow him. Now all they had to do was follow the rippling stream to the Smalling town.

It would be easy.

But not that easy.

Emily seemed to find the forest as dark as the street-tunnels. She tripped over stones and tree roots, and Muncle had to hold her hand again to stop her from grazing her knees and twisting her ankles. At the foot of the mountain where the trees thinned out, the sky became lighter. Muncle quickened his step.

"Slow down, Muncle," puffed Emily. "I can't keep up."

"Sorry, but we've got to hurry. If I'm not back in Puglug's room when she wakes up, they'll guess I've had something to do with your escape—and it's dawn already."

"That's not dawn," said Emily. "The sun comes up

on the other side of your mountain. It's just our street-lights. Look."

They had reached the fence that marked the entrance to the Smalling world. Ahead of them a brilliant torch with no flames burned on top of a pole. How did they do that without magic? Muncle shrank back into the shadows.

"You don't need to come any farther," Emily said. "My house is just there. Thank you for rescuing me, Muncle. I'll never forget it. I'll never forget *you*."

She was leaving. Muncle swallowed hard. "Emily, promise me you won't tell anyone where you've been."

"Why not?" Emily cried, her blue eyes wide. "Everyone will be so excited. They don't even know giants exist!"

"And they *mustn't* know. That's the whole point. We're only safe from your people because they've for-gotten about us. If you tell them we're still here, it will be like the old days and they'll use their magic to kill us again."

"Muncle, I've *told* you, there's no such thing as magic."

"They'll still kill us, whatever you call it."

Emily thought about this. "Maybe," she said. "But

I think they'd be more likely to put you in a zoo or something, nowadays."

Muncle didn't know what a zoo was, but it didn't sound good. "Promise me, Emily," he said firmly, "or I'll have to take you back to Puglug. I can't risk you giving us away. I have to think about my ma and pa, my brother and sister."

"And I have to think about *you*," she said quietly. "I don't want anyone to hurt *you*. But I shall have to tell them *something*. I can't just pretend I don't know where I've been. They'll want to know."

Muncle wanted to know, too.

"So, where were you all that time?" he asked. "How did Gri—I mean, how did those boys manage to kidnap you?"

"There was just one of them at first, a giant with three warts one on top of another dangling from his left ear like an earring. I was playing, just over there—on that tree with a swing. He came from nowhere, caught me in a big net, and . . . and . . . and . . ." Emily's voice was choked by sudden sobs.

So it *was* Gritt. How could he do such a thing? Muncle had to know the truth.

"And?" he said gently.

"Then he carried me into the forest, dumped me in an old hut, and blocked the door with a big rock. He kept me there till yesterday morning, when he took me through a gate in the mountainside to his horrible friend."

"A hut? With a door hanging off its hinges and a hole in the roof?"

"And millions of spiders, yes."

"My den," said Muncle. He felt like crying himself. He'd thought the hut was his own secret place, but of course anyone following the stream would have found it, too. "If it hadn't been for my exams I'd have been there yesterday. I could have rescued you."

Emily dashed her tears aside with the back of her hand. "Never mind," she said. "You've rescued me now. Muncle, I've got to go. Mom and Dad must be really worried."

Muncle grabbed her hand. "Can't you say you fell down an old mineshaft in the forest and it's taken you till now to climb out?"

"Well . . . I suppose I could. Or I could pretend I lost my memory. I'll think of something."

Muncle hugged her.

"Help, Muncle, you're crushing me!"

"Sorry!" Muncle let her go and smiled his broad, yellow smile. "I didn't think. It must feel just like it does when Ma hugs me."

"Is it very hard being a small giant?" Emily asked.

"Usually," Muncle admitted. "But today being small's been really useful."

As Emily turned to go, he felt empty and disappointed. Biblos would be disappointed, too. Muncle hadn't managed to discover a single Smalling secret.

"Wait!" He caught up with her just before she stepped out under the streetlight. "There's something I need to ask you." He pulled the Book out of his pocket and held it out to her. "Can you read this?"

"Oh, that book again," said Emily. She took it and thumbed through the pages.

"Be careful!" Muncle said anxiously. "It's old and valuable and as fragile as winter leaves."

"It doesn't look very valuable to me," Emily said. "It's just someone's favorite recipes. It *is* old, though. People don't do beautiful writing like this anymore."

Recipes? For Smalling spells?

"What sort of recipes?" Muncle asked eagerly.

"Cookies, cakes . . ." Emily handed the Book back with a laugh. "Nicer than the one your King had for his birthday."

Muncle stood openmouthed. Was it really only a recipe book? Surely not.

"I must go, Muncle."

Muncle shook off his shock. He wondered what Biblos would have to say about this. "You will remember not to tell, won't you? Promise?"

"I promise."

Emily ran to her gate and raised her hand once before opening it. She was safe.

Muncle hurriedly stuffed the Book into his pocket and made his way back into the cover of the forest. Behind him Smalling cries rang out. He couldn't tell whether they were cries of surprise or delight or anger, but he knew they meant that Emily was back where she belonged—with her ma and pa. Suddenly he felt tired out. He began to plod wearily uphill toward home.

Swoosh! Something whizzed past his left ear.

Swoosh! Another past his right ear.

Arrows!

Had Emily broken her promise already? Were the Smallings after him? Or had someone been watching him? He dropped to the ground and dragged himself under a bush.

Behind him came thwacking sounds. Someone was beating through the undergrowth with a stick. Muncle held his breath.

Then a hand fell on his shoulder and yanked him out of the bush.

SEVENTEEN

"Muncle!"

"Pa! What are you doing here?"

"Hunting, of course. I've got to earn every nugglin I can. If Gritt's found guilty, we may need to pay to get him out of the dungeons. The question is, what are *you* doing here? I could have killed you. I thought you were a deer."

"I thought *you* were a Smalling," said Muncle. He suddenly felt wobbly all over.

"A Smalling?" said Pa. "Firing arrows? If I'd had a magic killing stick, you'd be dead, my boy. And you haven't answered my question. What are you doing here? We thought you were in the palace helping the Princess with that Smalling. Ma hoped you'd be able to remind the King that he still owes us the fifty nugget prize for our play. That would go a long way to buying Gritt's freedom."

Muncle was too tired to make up a clever excuse for being in the forest. "I . . . I can't explain just now, Pa," he said. "It's a secret."

Pa drew his own conclusions. "You don't mean . . ." His voice dropped to an excited whisper, "the King's Secret Service?"

"I can't say, Pa." A thought struck him. "How late is it? I need to get back to the palace before the Princess wakes up and . . . er . . . needs me."

Pa chuckled with delight. "Well, well, my lad working for the Secret Service. But you look all tuckered out, Muncle. Do you want a lift back? It's time I was getting home anyway. It's nearly dawn and Ma will have the porridge on soon."

"Oh, yes, Pa. I've haven't had enough sleep, and I haven't had much to eat, either."

Pa swung Muncle onto his shoulders and delved in his sack.

"Here," he said, passing up a bloodied carcass. "Have a jackdaw or two. They're better grilled, of course, but they're not bad raw."

"Thanks."

Muncle tore off most of the feathers, and the rest just slipped down with the meat. He spat out the biggest bones and wiped his fingers on Pa's hair.

"What's that noise?" he whispered.

"You. Chewing."

"No, I've finished chewing. It's something else."

"Must be another hunter. Though most of them are too tired to be out the night of the King's Birthday."

There was an eerie call.

"Was that an owl?" asked Muncle.

"No." Pa became unusually still.

Eh-eh-ee!

"There it is again."

Muncle gripped Pa's neck.

Em-i-ly! Em-i-ly!

No mistaking it this time.

"Smallings," hissed Pa. "Looking for that girl. I've never heard them in the forest before."

"But . . ."

Something had gone wrong. Emily was safely home. Had she broken her promise? No, if they knew she was at home they wouldn't be calling her name. This must be a search party that hadn't yet heard she was safe.

"But what?" whispered Pa.

"Nothing. Pa, they're getting closer, and they're beating down bushes. If they find the ones outside our gates . . ."

"They still can't get in," said Pa. "They'd need a key."

"No, they wouldn't. One of the gates is broken, Pa—a Smalling could squeeze through. And that gate is the nearest one to where we are now."

Pa broke into a lumbering trot.

"Got to warn everyone," he puffed. "Got to call out the King's Guard. Where's this broken gate?"

"The lock's so rusty your key may not work, and I'm not leaving you on the outside with Smallings coming. Use your usual gate."

Pa changed direction, dodging in and out of the

trees. In a few minutes they were outside Pa's gate and quickly through to the other side. As soon as the gate was safely locked behind them, Pa broke into a run again, Muncle bouncing up and down on his shoulders.

"Where . . . are . . . you . . . going?" Muncle gasped.

"To the palace, of course. To warn the King."

Muncle thought quickly. "I have to get back to Puglug's room first. Can you take me to the dressing room under the stage?"

"A secret entrance! Brilliant!"

Pa raced across the deserted Crater and ducked into the space below the stage.

Muncle jumped down. "Open this hatch for me, will you, Pa?"

"But that's the ale-warming cellar," said Pa. He was clearly disappointed.

"That's why it's so clever. No one would ever guess. And you won't tell anyone, will you, Pa? About the secret entrance, or meeting me in the forest?"

"Hunter's honor," said Pa, lifting the trapdoor with one hand. "*Now* can I knock on the palace door?"

"Fetch Biblos from the museum first. That will give

me enough time to get to Puglug's room. And the King will want to talk to him anyway, before he gives orders to his Guard."

Pa closed the trapdoor and Muncle slid down the ramp. This time he had no candle to help him, but he had no Emily to slow him down, either, and it wasn't long before he pushed his way through the dragon flap back into the Princess's bedroom.

Puglug and Nursie were still snoring. The fire had gone out. An eye-watering smell suggested that Draggly had wet his bed. There was no way Muncle was going to share his basket now. But he was exhausted. He had to lie down somewhere. It was almost morning, but he had time for a little nap, and the thought of sheepskin blankets was just too tempting. He'd be all right, as long as he got up quickly the moment he heard Puglug stir. He felt his way to the dolls' bed and slid between the layers of fluffy fleece. . . .

"Good morning, Ugly Thing," trilled Puglug, whipping off Muncle's blankets. "How are you this mor—*Aaaagh!*"

Muncle opened his eyes to find Puglug bending

over him. Her pigtails had unraveled, and her eyebrows had disappeared into her bangs with surprise.

"Where's Ugly Thing?" she demanded. "What are you doing in her bed?"

It took Muncle a few moments to fully wake up. Nursie was still snoring like a dragon.

"I . . . I must have sleepwalked," he stammered. "I do that sometimes."

Puglug hauled him out of the bed and pulled the sheepskins off one after another. Muncle was astonished at how many there were. No wonder the bed was so soft.

"She's not here," said Puglug, shaking out the last sheepskin.

"Of course she's not here," said Muncle. "I wouldn't have got into the bed if there had been someone in it already."

"Then where is she?"

"How should I know? Maybe she walks in her sleep, too."

Puglug seized Muncle by the shoulders and shook him. "You weren't supposed to be sleeping!" she screamed, her sharp teeth terrifyingly close to his face. "You were here to guard her."

"No, I wasn't," said Muncle, looking at the nurse. Surely Puglug's screams must wake her up? "I was here to help you understand what she said. And as she didn't talk in her sleep, I was free to sleep, too."

"How dare you answer My Royal Hugeness back!" said the Princess, trying to unscrew Muncle's head from his neck.

He was saved by the King, who suddenly burst into Puglug's bedroom wearing nothing but a long knitted shirt and a sheepskin night-crown soft enough to sleep in.

"Emergency!" he cried. "Doom! Disaster! There's a Smalling alert!"

EIGHTEEN

Puglug let go of Muncle and turned tearfully to her pa.

"I know!" she said. "It's awful."

"You *know*?" exclaimed the King. "Who told you?"

"No one. I found out for myself, when I came to wake her up."

Muncle slung his bag over his shoulder, ready to leave. With Emily gone, his job in the palace was over. But King Thortless was not thinking about jobs. "What are you talking about?" he said.

"The Smalling. Ugly Thing. She's gone."

"Gone?"

"Disappeared. In the night."

"Oh, doom and double doom!" cried the King.

He shook Nursie, who was *still* snoring.

"Chundering chilbugs!" the old woman exclaimed, pushing him roughly away. Then she realized who it was, staggered sleepily out of her chair, and collapsed on the floor in a failed curtsy.

"Sleeping on the job, Nursie?" the King yelled. "Get up and take the Princess to the Royal Stables immediately. Puglug, you're to stay hidden there until the all clear is sounded. Your ma's down there already."

"In the smelly old stables?" Puglug said. "Why?"

"Smallings advancing. National emergency. Safest place to hide. No, there's no time to get dressed. Nursie, you take her clothes, and some cushions and blankets to make her comfortable. Now give me that minikin, Puglug. I want him!"

Muncle went rigid with fear. Had Pa accidentally given him away?

"But I want him myself," complained Puglug. "He can be my new pet, now that Ugly Thing is gone."

"The Wise Man wants to question him, my precious. You can have him back as soon as the emergency's over."

"Oh, all right. Catch."

Puglug picked Muncle up and tossed him to her father, who juggled with him for a moment before clamping him once again under his arm.

Dizzily, Muncle tried to gather his thoughts. How much trouble was he in? Would life in the dungeons be worse than life as Puglug's pet?

The King carried him swiftly to the palace entrance hall and dumped him down in front of Biblos.

The Wise Man was sitting miserably on a bench carved in the shape of a sleeping dragon. His long hair was bundled under a nightcap and his long beard into a beardcap, but he was wearing his normal robe. His knobbly hands were folded on top of his stick, and his chin was propped on top of his hands. Pa was bending over him, hands on his knees, saying something about Gritt.

"Where's the girl?" said Biblos, turning his attention immediately to the King. "Holding her to ransom in exchange for our lives is our only hope."

"We haven't got the girl, Wise Man. It appears she's escaped."

"What?" gasped Biblos. "With Nursie keeping watch

in the Princess's room and guards on the palace doors? Muncle, you were there. However did she manage to escape?"

"I don't *know*," Muncle said, thinking on his feet, "but I can guess."

"You *can*?"

Biblos and the King leaned toward him eagerly.

"There's only one possible explanation," said Muncle. He paused for effect. "She must have used Smalling magic!"

"But she told us there was no such thing," said the King.

"She was trying to trick us," said Biblos. "You can't believe anything she said, Your Enormity. It was all nonsense, like this mountain blowing itself up. What did she call it? A 'volcano'?"

"That's it!" cried Muncle, as Emily's words suddenly came back to him:

One day this mountain will burst open, and flames and melted rock will gush out of it.

"That's how we can defend ourselves. All we have to do is make the Smallings think that Mount Grumble *is* blowing up, and they'll run away."

Biblos shook his head. "Muncle, mountains can't blow themselves up. The Smallings will never fall for it."

"*We* know mountains can't blow themselves up," Muncle said—although he'd been wondering about this more and more—"but the Smallings believe they *can*. It's such a silly idea that Emily couldn't have thought of it if she hadn't heard it before."

"Well, I suppose it's worth a try," said Biblos. "I've no ideas myself. Yours is the only one we've got."

The King sat down on the dragon bench beside Biblos and pushed his night-crown back to scratch his head. "But how are we going to make it look as if Mount Grumble is a blowing-up 'volcano' thingy?"

"Beats me." Biblos sighed.

"Flames have got to burst out of it," said Muncle, "and we can do flames easily enough. Dragons can set fire to things."

"Not whole mountains," said Biblos.

"It doesn't need to be the whole mountain. Just enough trees to make the Smallings *think* it's the whole mountain."

"Of course!" cried the King. "My Dragon Division can set the forest on fire!"

"It wasn't just fire, though, was it?" said Biblos. "Wasn't there something about melting rock? Our dragons aren't hot enough for that."

Muncle thought for a moment. "Snarg might be. He's had way more sun than the others."

"But we haven't *got* Snarg," Pa pointed out. "You lost him again."

"I know," said Muncle. "For my idea to work, I've got to catch him."

He fumbled in his bag and found his dragon flute.

"A school flute?" said Biblos. "That sound won't carry very far. You'd better have mine."

He unfastened a flute that hung from one of the links on his chain of office. It was silver, inlaid with intricate gold patterns, and its little chain was just the right length to fit around Muncle's neck.

"It's beautiful!" gasped Muncle, quite overwhelmed that Biblos was lending him such a precious thing. "Even Mr. Thwackum's flute hasn't got patterns on it. I'll take good care of it and bring it straight back."

"No, no," said Biblos. "You must keep it. A dragon rider needs a decent flute. And I've no need of it. I haven't had my own dragon for years."

He fished in his pocket and pulled out a copper token. Muncle saw that it was a tiny copy of the donkey badge on Biblos's chain of office.

"Go and catch Snarg at once," said the Wise Man. "Give this donkey token to anyone who challenges you, to prove you have permission to leave the town. Trogg, here's another one for you."

"I don't need one." Pa pointed to the hunter's badge on his jerkin. "I already have permission to leave."

Biblos shook his head. "Your token is to give to the Captain of the Guard. I want you to take him my orders. It'll be quicker than me sending for him. Tell him to march the Dragon Division into the forest and set fire to it at once."

"Only a bit of it," said Muncle hurriedly. "We need the rest of the trees to hide the dragons and their handlers, or the Smallings will know it's not a volcano."

Pa paused for a moment, looking with pride at the token in his hand.

"Come on, Pa, let's get going. There's no time to lose."

"You don't need me, do you?" said the King, edging away. "I . . . er . . . think I ought to go to the stables—to look after my family, I mean."

"We've all got families . . . ," began Pa.

". . . and the King's right, we must look after them," Muncle interrupted, before Pa could say anything rude. "It's most important to keep our King and Royal Family safe," he added, when Biblos failed to say anything helpful. "But first have the Town Crier sound the alarm, so that everyone else knows to hide in their stables, too."

Who could guess, with Smallings approaching, whether it would be safer to hide or run? Making people *feel* safe was probably the best they could do.

NINETEEN

"I'll carry you to the gate," said Pa, as two footmen heaved open the palace door to let them out.

"Just let me try something first," said Muncle. "This might be even quicker."

He put his new flute to his lips and blew "come here." He only had to blow once. The shrill signal echoed around the Crater walls. Long before it died away, Snarg appeared through the cloud and circled overhead. But he didn't land.

"Put your club down, Pa," said Muncle. "I think it may be reminding him of Mr. Thwackum."

Pa threw his hunting club on the ground and stepped away from it.

Snarg was still taking no chances. He landed well out of reach, on top of one of the grandstands. Muncle scrambled up the steep rows of seats. When he reached Snarg, the dragon stretched out his neck and gave him a welcoming lick. His tongue singed the hairs off Muncle's chin and shriveled a couple of his warts.

"Aaah!" he yelped, but it was a promising sign. Snarg's breath was good and hot. "See you later, Pa!" he shouted, climbing quickly onto the dragon's back.

As Snarg lifted off, Muncle looked down. Pa stood openmouthed and rooted to the spot. Then he pulled himself together, picked up his club, and began to run. A few moments later the Crater gong sounded the emergency alarm.

Bong! Bong! Bong! Bong! Bong!

Muncle took Snarg straight up through the cloud again for an extra feed of sunshine, and waited for the Dragon Division to fill the forest with smoke. In the distance he could hear the shrill sounds of dragon flutes and the occasional crack of a whip. Soon he smelled burning, and heard the hiss and crackle of flames far below.

It was time to put Snarg to work.

He circled lower. Somewhere down here, Pa had once said, was a cliff which dropped straight down to the Smalling town. With all the smoke it wasn't easy to find, and he didn't want to waste all Snarg's fiery breath in the wrong spot! The melted rock had to trickle down the side of the mountain that faced the town to make the Smallings think the volcano was erupting.

At last, a gust of wind parted the smoke and gave him a brief glimpse of Smalling roofs. He was in the right place.

"Sit!" Muncle blew urgently, afraid the growing wind might part the smoke again and reveal them to the Smallings, who must by now have noticed the fire in the forest.

Snarg landed behind some large, jagged boulders on the cliff top, safely out of sight of the town.

"Now . . . burn," said Muncle, and blew the command.

Snarg twisted his neck all the way around and gave Muncle a puzzled look.

"I know it doesn't look as if there's anything here that *will* burn, Snarg, but I want you to try. Burn the *rock*. Burn! Burn!"

He blew the signal for "burn" again and again. It was the best he could do. There was no signal for "melt."

Snarg turned away and waited for a more sensible instruction. When none came, he lay his head down beside a boulder and settled in for a rest. He yawned. His great jaws opened wide and flames poured out. The rock by his nose glowed pink and reflected warmth back at him. He snuggled up to it and sighed contentedly. The sigh was hotter than the yawn, and the rock glowed red.

"That's it, Snarg!" said Muncle excitedly. "Just keep doing that!"

But there was no signal for "sigh," either. Instead, Muncle blew the signal for "stay." Then he slid to the ground, ran to the nearest bushes, and gathered an armful of branches and leaves. He spread them in front of Snarg's nose, and blew "burn" again.

Now the dragon had no problem following orders. He let out a single puff. The branches flared up for a moment and then shriveled to a tiny pile of ash. The boulder underneath turned white, and a tiny trickle of goo oozed out.

"Yes!" cried Muncle. "You *can* do it!"

What a relief. He'd been afraid that even Snarg wouldn't be hot enough to melt rock. He slapped the dragon on the leg by way of congratulation and encouragement.

"Now burn, burn, burn!" he urged.

But with no more branches to burn and the rock now soft and warm, the dragon dozed off. Far below them, Muncle could hear high-pitched voices that could only be Smallings. He'd got to make them think that this was a volcano, and not just a forest fire, or they might try to put it out instead of running away.

He tried something else. Fetching another armful of branches, he put them right on the edge of the cliff. All but the longest one. With that, he reached out from a safe distance and tickled the dragon's left nostril.

Waaah-chooo!

Snarg jumped and let out the most enormous sneeze. Flame and smoke shot from his nose and mouth with a roar that frightened even Muncle. The branches flew blazing into the air. The boulders at the cliff top, already softened, turned into hot red lava and started to trickle down the mountainside.

Muncle hurriedly backed away, afraid that Snarg might melt the bit of cliff he was standing on, too. He edged along until he found a place where it was safer to peer over. Smoke hid a lot of the view, but as it wafted apart, he glimpsed the effect of Snarg's sneeze.

Sparks had reached the fence that separated the forest from the Smalling town, and flames were beginning to creep along it.

Snarg, clearly impressed with what he'd achieved, woke up properly and coughed and snorted at more of the cliff top. Weakened and smoldering, it broke away beneath him. Hurriedly he took to his wings.

"Come here!" Muncle whistled urgently, but Snarg didn't come. Instead he circled upward in search of a fresh supply of sunshine. Muncle blew his flute till he was out of breath and Snarg was out of earshot. It was too late.

The dragon was lost. For the third time.

For a few moments Muncle thought the shrill sound he could now hear was just the memory of the dragon

flute ringing in his ears. Then he recognized it for what it was.

Smalling screams.

He peered over the cliff again. The fence near Emily's house was blazing now. He hoped she would be all right.

TWENTY

Muncle watched from the cliff top as Smallings raced out of the forest and down the alley into the wider road at the far end. As they ran past, doors and gates opened, and Smallings from the houses joined them, all running to get into carts that whooshed them away. His plan was working! The Smallings thought the volcano was erupting. He sighed with relief. The giants were safe.

But his relief didn't last long.

Suddenly there was the roaring of excited giants.

And the bellowing of dragons.

The soldiers of the Dragon Division were going to give themselves away while the last of the Smallings were still within earshot!

Muncle had to stop the battle—before the Smallings realized it *was* a battle.

He stumbled through the scrubby trees on the cliff top and headed downhill into the thick of the forest. Thankfully the soldiers had started the fire well away from the town gates, but the whole forest was full of horribly thick smoke. With watering eyes, Muncle coughed and blundered his way through it, searching every clump of bramble and ivy for a gate into Mount Grumble.

Then he realized something. He didn't have to waste time asking Biblos or the King to order the retreat. He still had the copper donkey token. He could use it to stop the battle himself. No one would know that wasn't why he'd been given it.

He turned and charged blindly in the direction of giant rumbles and dragon roars, tripped over a tree root, and hit something big and bulky.

"Help!" cried the Captain of the King's Guard. "Get those dragons back here, men. They're attacking from behind!"

"What?" said Muncle, untangling himself from the folds of the Captain's uniform. "Attacking? Where?"

The Captain threw him to the ground and pinned him down. "Help!" he yelled again. "I've taken a prisoner. Backup needed! I repeat: Backup needed!"

Muncle opened his mouth, but no sound came out. The Captain had squashed all the breath out of his lungs. A soldier ran out of the smoke with a flaming sapling in his hand.

"Where are the rest of them?" he cried. "The next one's mine!"

Then he saw Muncle.

"That's not a Smalling, Captain," he said. He sounded disappointed. "That's the minikin who was in that funny act yesterday. He just *pretends* to be a Smalling."

"*Pretends?*" cried the Captain, picking Muncle up and shaking the breath back into him. "This is no time for playacting, lad. Don't you know there's a war on?"

"I'm sorry," said Muncle, "I just haven't had a chance to change back into my own clothes yet."

"Then you shouldn't be wandering around in the forest," said the soldier. "We could have killed you."

"You shouldn't be wandering around in the forest

anyway," snapped the Captain. "I'll report you to the King as soon as the battle's over."

"But that's what I came to tell you," said Muncle. "The battle *is* over. The Wise Man wants you to go back to the Crater at once."

He pulled the token from his pocket and handed it to the Captain.

The disappointed soldier peered at it closely. "You mean we should retreat?" he said. "But we've hardly started."

"The Smallings have run away. We've done enough."

"We?" The Captain snorted. "Well, I've certainly done *my* part, but I don't think *you* can take much credit, minikin. Anyone can carry messages, and anyone *else* would have had the sense not to do it disguised as a Smalling."

"Please, just tell your soldiers," said Muncle. "The King will be furious if you burn down so much of the forest that his hunters can't find him any meat."

"Meat!" cried the soldier. He flung his burning sapling to the ground and trampled the flames out with his bare feet. Then he ran after the rest of the Dragon Division.

"Retreat!" he yelled. "Save the meat. Retreat! Save the meat!"

It had worked! Nobody had questioned why Biblos had given such an important order to a small boy. A copper token no bigger than a nugglin was all it took to turn the Dragon Division around and send them home.

He had done it.

Now all he wanted to do was go home.

Muncle tried again to find his broken town gate. But none of the gates was covered with bramble patches anymore. The Dragon Division had torn everything up as they charged around setting fire to things, and there were a dozen soldiers guarding every gate now, each with enough spears, battle-axes, and truncheons for a whole army. As Muncle approached, a hail of arrows flew in his direction.

He threw himself flat on his face.

"Don't shoot!" he shouted. "I'm not a Smalling."

A spear landed within a thumb's width of his right elbow.

"I'm not a Smalling!" he yelled again. "I'm just Hunter Trogg's son, the minikin from yesterday's play."

It was the first time he'd ever used the word "minikin."

Ma wouldn't allow it to be spoken at home. She insisted he still had plenty of time to grow. But it was the word everyone else used, and just now it was the quickest and easiest way to explain who he was and avoid being chopped in two by a battle-ax.

"Prove it!" the guard yelled back.

"I'm grimy and warty. Smallings are clean and smooth." Muncle thought quickly. "And if I was a Smalling I wouldn't have heard of Hunter Trogg."

The rattle of arrows was replaced by a mutter of voices.

"All right," one of them said. "Get up and come over here slowly. Keep your hands above your head."

Muncle did as he was told.

"Recite the Law," said the guard who seemed to be slightly more in charge than any of the others.

"*Smallings are evil,*" said Muncle, "*Smallings are mean, Smallings would kill our King and—*"

"Name!"

"Muncle Trogg."

"Not *your* name, wibblewit, the *King's* name."

"Oh. Thortless the Thirteenth."

They let him in.

TWENTY-ONE

Muncle hardly recognized Mount Grumble. Every torch was out. Every street-tunnel was silent. The giants were hiding behind the iron doors of their guard-dragon stables. The sooner Muncle could get the good news to the King and Biblos, the sooner the Town Crier could sound the all clear to let the whole town know. But he was exhausted now, and strangely tearful. He plodded very slowly through the dark street-tunnels.

When he reached the Crater, though, he felt a sense of relief. He wondered if he was beginning to get used to daylight. He looked up to check there was enough cloud cover to hide Snarg from the fleeing Smallings.

"Ma!" he cried. "Pa! Whatever are you doing up there?"

High on the top of the grandstand, at the point where he and Snarg had taken off, Ma, Pa, and Flubb sat gazing anxiously into the sky.

"Mumble!" called Flubb, jigging about excitedly in her baby basket.

Pa charged down the steps three at a time.

"Muncle!" he cried. "We were expecting you to come back the same way you went."

Ma puffed down after Pa and took Muncle into one of her massive hugs.

"You're safe," she said, her tears dripping into Muncle's hair. "But where's the dragon? I was hoping to see you ride him home."

"Lost again, I'm afraid," said Muncle, as soon as Ma loosened her grip enough for him to breathe. "But it doesn't matter, because there's no one to see him. The trick worked. The Smallings have run away in their whooshing carts."

"You mean we've won the battle?" cried Pa.

"Well, it wasn't a battle, exactly—"

"If the Dragon Division is out, it's war!" Pa grabbed Muncle and swung him high in the air. "And it was all your idea. You deserve a reward. You deserve the King's Medal!"

"The King! I haven't told him yet. I need to go to the palace at once."

"I'll take you," said Pa, sitting Muncle on his shoulders. "There's something I want to say to the King, too."

"And me," said Ma, bustling across the Crater behind them.

"Thanks," said Muncle. "It'd be good if you were there. You can protect me from Puglug."

"The Princess?" chortled Ma. "That sweet little thing? What could she possibly do to you?"

"Keep me as a pet." Muncle shuddered in horror as he remembered Puglug's kisses.

"Keep you?" said Ma. "At the palace? Is that a job? Would you get paid? Because if so—"

"Muncle doesn't need a job," said Pa. "He's already got one. In the King's Secret Service."

"What?" gasped Ma.

"No, no, Pa," Muncle said hurriedly. "That was just for last night and you mustn't mention it to anybody . . ."

But Pa had stopped listening. He galloped across the Crater and hammered on the palace door. It took a long time for anyone to answer, and when someone did, Muncle was surprised to find it was not a guard, but Biblos.

"He's done it!" cried Pa, before either Muncle or Biblos could say a word. "My boy's done it! He's made the Smallings run away. You *will* tell the King to give him a reward, won't you? It's the least he deserves. After all, *he* had the idea when you didn't."

"*Pa!* You can't be rude to the Wise Man!" Muncle was shocked.

But Biblos's weary eyes lit up. "No, no, Muncle," he said, making his way back to the dragon bench, "your pa's quite right. I will certainly tell the King he should reward you. Just pull that bell cord, will you? It will ring in the Royal Stables. Two tugs, then a pause, over and over again. Just like the all clear on the town gong."

Muncle tugged twice and paused, tugged twice and paused, until a footman peered nervously around a door. He looked surprised to find such a shabby family in the grand entrance hall.

"The King wants to know if that was the all clear or the lunch bell," he said.

"The all clear, of course," said Biblos. "The Dragon Division has driven the Smallings away. Tell the Royal Family they can come out of hiding."

The footman disappeared, and a short time later two bodyguards marched in, followed at a safe distance by the King.

"Splendid news, Biblos!" he said, without even glancing at the Troggs. "Giants have beaten the Smallings again, and it happened while I was on the throne. I'll be the most important king in history."

He sat down beside Biblos and slapped the old man on the back, nearly knocking him off the bench. "And *you'll* be the most important Wise Man," he added.

Biblos shook his head. "Not me, Your Enormity," he said, waving his ear trumpet toward Muncle. "It wasn't my idea."

The King noticed the Trogg family for the first time.

"What are these people doing here?" he said.

Ma and Pa spoke at the same time.

"I'm here to ask for a medal for my son, Muncle," said Pa.

"I'm here to ask for a pardon for my son, Gritt," said Ma.

"A meddon for their son Grincle?" said the King, turning back to Biblos. "What are they talking about, Wise Man?"

But Biblos didn't hear him. He'd put his ear trumpet down so that he could lift the heavy chain of office from around his neck.

"What are you doing?" cried the King.

Biblos had his ear trumpet back in place. "Resigning, Your Enormity. I'm not your Wise Man anymore. I'm too old for this job. At last I can retire. I've lost my ideas and someone else has found them. I think you should appoint . . . Muncle Trogg, in my place."

"Who?" The King looked puzzled.

"My boy!" cried Pa, plonking Muncle down in front of the King. "That's who. My boy!"

"No, really," gasped Muncle, "I couldn't possibly, I . . ."

"Think of the money!" Pa hissed in Muncle's ear.

"But I failed my Gigantia!"

Biblos looked rather embarrassed.

"Ah, yes," he said. "Your Gigantia. I'm afraid there was rather a miscarriage of justice there. The truth of the matter is that you were such an expert in Dragon Science and Smalling Studies that our marking system couldn't cope. I shall, of course, see to it that the school curriculum is changed. I mean, *you* will see to it, as our new Wise Man."

"But he's a minikin," spluttered the King.

"He may have a small body, sire, but he has big ideas and great courage. If it hadn't been for his 'volcano' plan, Mount Grumble would be overrun with Smallings by now."

King Thortless chuckled. "Oh, yes—the 'volcano'! Those silly Smallings will believe anything." Then he turned and looked down at Muncle doubtfully.

"If I did make you Wise Man," he said, "what would be your first piece of advice?"

"Have the all clear sounded, sire," said Muncle. "And then have the Steward of Your Enormity's Birthday organize an extra day of fun and feasting to celebrate our victory."

"Feasting!" cried the King. "*Excellent* idea. Biblos, I agree. I hereby announce that the minikin—"

A door at the back of the hall burst open. Puglug, in a splendid fleece dress trimmed with sheep-poo tassels, pulled away from Nursie, barged past her father, and swept Muncle into her arms.

"Mine!" she shouted.

TWENTY-TWO

"No, Pugling dear," said the King, removing Muncle from the Princess's arms by force. "I'm afraid he's not yours."

"But you promised!" Puglug stamped both feet. "You said I could have him back after the emergency—and this *is* after the emergency."

"Yes, my precious, but things have changed. Don't worry, you'll be seeing plenty of the minikin in the future, that I can promise you. Now go and play with your other toys and I'll get you a new pet very soon.

We've lots to choose from now that the Smallings have gone. How about a pig?"

"I don't know what a pig's like," said Puglug sulkily.

"It's smooth and pink," Pa said helpfully. "I saw one once when I was raiding a Smalling farm."

"Like Ugly Thing, you mean?"

"Yes," said Muncle quickly. "Just like Ugly Thing."

"Oh," said Puglug, and she went away happy.

"How clever of you to know that," said King Thortless. "Biblos has never once told me that pigs looked like Smallings. You must become my new Wise Man right away."

He took the chain of office from Biblos and hung it round Muncle's neck. It reached to his knees.

"It'll have to be shortened," said the King. "Give it back to me and I'll send it to my goldsmith."

"No need for that," said Pa quickly. "I can shorten it."

The King eyed him suspiciously. "Very well," he said, "but make sure you bring every spare link of gold back here. They belong to me. Now, Wise Man—Biblos, I mean. Where are you going to live when you retire?"

"Oh, Biblos, please don't leave the museum," said Muncle. "I wouldn't want that. I'll come and work there every day, because I'll need your help, but I'd like to go on living at home with Ma and Pa."

"Does that suit you, Biblos?" asked the King.

"Oh, yes, Your Enormity," said the old man. "That suits me very well indeed." He reached into his pocket and brought out a handful of donkey tokens. "Here, Muncle, you'll be needing these."

The tokens filled the little pockets of the Smalling trousers, leaving no room for anything else.

"Can you make a special purse for me to keep them in, Ma?" Muncle said. "Ma? Why are you crying?"

Ma pulled a handful of hair loose from her bun and blew her nose on it.

"I'm just so happy," she sobbed, "or at least I would be, if it wasn't for—"

Muncle suddenly had another idea, and it wasn't one he wanted to share with Biblos or the King.

"Will you excuse us now, please, Your Enormity?" he said before Ma could get to the end of her sentence. "I'm really rather tired. It was hard work, making a volcano."

"Of course, of course," said the King. "I'll take your advice and have the Town Crier announce a feast immediately."

"And the all clear, Your Enormity. He should sound that first."

"The all clear first. And then the feast. Right. Got it. Thank you. And I look forward to getting your next piece of advice, Wise Minikin."

"Wise *Man*," said Pa sharply.

"Sorry," said the King. "This is going to take a bit of getting used to."

"You can say that again," said Muncle.

"This is going to take a bit of getting used to," said the King.

"You shouldn't have interrupted me like that," said Ma the moment they were outside. "I was just going to ask the King about a pardon for Gritt."

"It's probably best if he doesn't know about it," said Muncle. "He might not be too keen on the idea."

"No, your ma's right," said Pa. "The King *may* not like it, but we've got to ask. We've got to ask for our prize money, too, so we can buy Gritt's freedom if he doesn't get pardoned. We can't leave him in the dungeons without trying everything."

"We're not *going* to leave him in the dungeons," said Muncle, waggling the chain of office that he'd tucked into his Smalling shirt. "I'm the Wise Man, remember? With all those donkey tokens, I can order Gritt's freedom myself."

Ma burst into tears all over again.

Pa grabbed Muncle, swung him onto his shoulders, and raced across the Crater once again, this time toward the Dungeon Guard House.

There was nobody there.

"Where the thrumbles is everyone?" said Pa.

"I expect the guards hid in the dungeons when they heard the alarm," said Muncle. "They're probably waiting for the all clear. We'll have to go down there ourselves."

Ma came puffing up behind them. Flubb had had enough of being bounced up and down on Ma's back, and had started to wail.

"Go down to the dungeons?" said Ma. "I don't think I can bear to see Gritt in there."

"Why don't you and Flubb wait here?" said Muncle. "We shouldn't be long."

He found a tinderbox on the Guard House shelf and lit a torch. The dungeons were deep in the bowels of the mountain, down three flights of very, very steep steps, beneath the Royal Stables. Pa carried Muncle on his back and Muncle held the torch. When they got halfway down the third flight of steps, an orange glow appeared ahead and they were hit by a wave of heat. It was even hotter in the dungeons than it was in the Dragon Farm.

At the bottom of the stairs was a second Guard House. There were bars in its iron door like those in Mr. Thwackum's office and, as Pa and Muncle approached, an array of spearheads and arrows were suddenly poked through them.

"Who goes there?"

"Hunter Trogg," said Pa, lowering Muncle to the ground. "The emergency's over and I've come with a pardon for my son."

There was a lot of muttering inside the Guard House.

"I know Trogg," one voice said. "Here, let me have a look."

One by one the spears and arrows were taken away and an eye appeared.

"Yes, that's him, you can unlock the door."

The Guard House door opened and Pa barged straight in. It was a narrow room, and the only way in or out of the dungeons was through another door at the far end. Four guards sat around in rather unusual uniforms, bare tattooed skin above the waist and breeches cut off well above the knee for coolness.

The Dungeon Master barred Pa's progress with a battle-ax.

"Token," he said, sweat dripping from his big red nose.

Muncle handed over a donkey token.

"Token," the Dungeon Master said again.

"But I've just given you one."

"That was for the Upper Guard House." The Dungeon Master ignored Muncle and spoke to Pa. "Now I want one for the Lower Guard House."

Muncle pulled another token from his pocket. The Dungeon Master looked taken aback. He took the token and bit on it before accepting it.

"All right, this way."

He opened the door at the far end and led Pa and Muncle into a corridor with rows of cells on either side. There was no need for torches. The orange glow was as bright as firelight. Where was it coming from? Muncle wondered.

The Dungeon Master walked along the corridor, knocking on each door with his battle-ax. At each knock the prisoner inside replied with his name. At the eighth door an unhappy little voice said, "Gritt Trogg."

"Visitors for you, Trogg," said the Dungeon Master. Then he turned to Pa. "Token," he said.

"What's this one for?" demanded Muncle. Getting Gritt out was harder than he'd expected.

"To open the door."

Muncle handed over another token. The Dungeon Master opened the door, and there was Gritt. Stark naked.

"Muncle!" he gasped. "Pa! Have they arrested you, too?"

"No!" cried Muncle joyfully. He jumped down from Pa's shoulders, rushed into the cell, and hugged as much of Gritt as he could reach. "We're here to take you home."

Pa turned angrily on the Dungeon Master. "What have you done with his clothes?" he demanded.

"Don't worry, Pa," said Gritt, hugging Muncle back surprisingly gently. "I took them off myself. It's thrumblin' hot in here."

The Dungeon Master laughed. "That's the central heating," he said. "It's all right once you get used to it, though even some of the guards have been complaining that it's a bit too hot lately."

Muncle studied the crack in the floor of Gritt's cell thoughtfully. Something that looked like orange toffee was oozing and heaving up from beneath. And the floor itself was almost too hot to touch. He hopped from foot to burning foot, but shivered in spite of the terrible heat.

Flames and melting rock, Emily had said.

"How long has this been happening?" he asked.

The Dungeon Master shrugged. "As long as I've worked here," he said. "Though it was only in two cells when I started, and now it's in most of them."

"Doesn't matter how many cells the heating's in," said Pa, "as long as our Gritt isn't in any of them. Get your clothes, lad. Ma and Flubb are waiting for you upstairs."

"Two tokens," said the Dungeon Master.

"But we've given you three already," said Pa.

"To release a prisoner"—he held up the fingers of one hand—"I need a total of five."

Muncle handed over two more tokens.

Gritt snatched up his clothes from a shadowy corner of his cell and dashed through the Lower Guard House and up the three flights of stairs before the Dungeon Master could change his mind. By the time Pa and Muncle caught up with him, Ma was giving him one of her rib-cracking hugs, and Flubb was wobbling with laughter.

"Git!" she chuckled, pointing delightedly at Gritt's equally wobbly bare bottom. "Git!"

"Get your clothes on, lad," said Pa. "I'm not taking you out like that and I want to get home and start celebrating. Tonight I'm going to hunt us an ox."

"An ox?" said Gritt. "A whole ox? To celebrate me getting out of the dungeons?"

"Well, he can hardly hunt us half an ox," said Muncle, and both boys giggled.

Out in the Crater the town gong started to boom.

"Is that lunchtime?" asked Gritt, hurriedly pulling on his breeches.

"It's the all clear," said Ma, smiling tearfully. "A lot of

things have happened while you've been . . . downstairs."

"What?" said Gritt. "What have I missed?"

"You tell him, Muncle," said Ma. "It's your story, really."

"I will tell you," Muncle agreed, as they followed Pa into the Crater, "but first I need to talk to Biblos." He wanted to know how much the old man knew about the Central Heating. He needed to tell him about the Book, too, though he was afraid of disappointing him.

"Now?" said Ma. "You deserve a holiday. Surely you don't need to start work until after the celebration feast?"

"I've started already, Ma," said Muncle seriously. "I'm working on a new idea right now. I think we ought to stop clipping dragon's wings, and train everybody to ride them."

He thought wistfully of Snarg. Would he ever see him again?

"Everybody?" cried Ma. "Even me? Whatever for?"

"Because if we need to leave Mount Grumble in a hurry, that will be the quickest way to go."

"But we'll never need to leave," said Pa. "Not now that we know how to beat the Smallings."

"I hope you're right," said Muncle, as doors opened

and relieved giants poured into the Crater, chattering with excitement as they waited for the Town Crier's next bulletin. He didn't want to leave Mount Grumble now—he was just beginning to feel he really belonged in the giants' world. "But I need to be sure."

"*You* need to be sure?" said Gritt, with a chuckle. "Since when does it matter what *you* think, *little* brother?" He grabbed Muncle playfully and swung him into the air by the ankles.

"Ma!" shrieked the Wise Man, as copper donkey tokens tumbled out of his pockets. "Gritt's upside-downing me AGAIN!"

Author Janet Foxley
Talks About Muncle Trogg

"You've won!"

It was hard to believe when I first got that phone call, and it's still hard to believe now. I'd been writing for thirty-five years, and working on *Muncle Trogg* on and off for about eight. But once I got over the shock of winning the third annual *Times of London*/Chicken House Children's Fiction Competition, I was overcome with not only excitement at the prospect of being published, but also a deep sense of satisfaction that my writing had been recognized by people who really knew about children's books—including Chicken House publisher Barry Cunningham, who is world-renowned for discovering J. K. Rowling.

I won the contest; then came the "life-changing" part. I had to learn to work on deadline as the story was edited: tidying up and strengthening the plot, then adding more touches of humor. While I wrestled with tiny giants and grumpy dragons, my husband nobly set about learning what the kitchen was for.

The excitement didn't end with publication in Great Britain. The American edition, published by Scholastic, soon followed, and there are twenty-one foreign editions planned so far: everything from Portuguese to Japanese to Polish! Just as thrilling—maybe even more so!—an animated motion-picture adaptation is also in the works. Just imagine seeing little Muncle on the big screen!

When I came to write *Muncle Trogg*, I wanted the book to have a traditional folktale element, and witches and wizards were already well represented in children's literature, so I chose giants instead. Once that was decided, it was obvious what my protagonist's problem was going to be: What could be worse for a boy giant than being small? When you first meet Muncle, he is being held upside down by his much bigger, and *younger*, brother Gritt. Then he's made fun of by all the other kid giants in his class. It's not until he goes on a school trip to the Smallings Museum, meets Biblos the Wise Man, and finds that he fits into human clothes that Muncle begins to get an idea about how being the runt of the giants could actually come in useful. But he's still surprised, after he ventures down to the foot of Mount Grumble for the very first time, to discover that Smallings don't walk around with their knuckles dragging on the ground!

Although he can't pass for human after all, Muncle makes friends with Emily, a clever girl who sees past appearances. So he has to think fast when, later, Gritt snatches up Emily and offers her on a silver platter as a birthday meal to the king! Muncle may be small, but he more than makes up for what he lacks in size with brains and bravery, saving his brother, his family, and ultimately the entire Mount Grumble community—and Emily, too.

Anyone who has ever been bullied, or who feels that they are different from everybody else, will relate to Muncle. Readers who might not yet know their own unique talents will, I hope, be encouraged by the fact that even Muncle turns out to be good at many things. And everyone should chuckle at the giants' taste and standards of behavior, which are rather different from our own—unless, that is, you also like to eat fungus porridge with cobwebs for breakfast!

When I was a child, the authors I liked were Arthur Ransome, who wrote the *Swallows and Amazons* series, and E. Nesbit, who is beloved for *The Railway Children*, her Bastables series, and so many other classics. I suppose big people and little people have always been in my thoughts, because the novel I most wish I'd written is *The Borrowers*, by Mary Norton. And I didn't stop reading children's stories once I was a grown-up: My own children are grown up now, too, but I read aloud to my son until he was thirteen, because he is dyslexic. That introduced me to a new generation of wonderful authors, and I knew that if I ever did write a book myself, it would be for young readers. To this day I like imagining different ways of life. But the giant success of the prize-winning Muncle has turned my own life into a fairy tale!

■ ■ ■

Janet Foxley is a retired administrator from Royal Holloway, University of London. She now lives with her husband in a village outside Carlisle, Cumbria, England. She recently finished writing The Flying Donkey, *Muncle Trogg's second adventure!* Friend her on Facebook, and visit her website, www.janetfoxley.co.uk.

ACKNOWLEDGMENTS

I am grateful to everyone who has helped Muncle on his way, including: Helen Corner and her Cornerstones team; Katherine Langrish, who guided his early steps; Belinda Hollyer, who pointed him in the right direction when he got lost; and Barry Cunningham and all the judges of *The Times*/Chicken House Children's Fiction Competition 2010, who thought Muncle should be introduced to a wider readership.

I should particularly like to thank everyone at the Chicken House for their support and enthusiasm, and especially Rachel Leyshon for her help with the plot and Imogen Cooper for her guidance on just about everything.

Last, and most of all, I should like to thank my husband Donald, daughter Rachel, and son Sebastian, who have for decades tolerated with good humour my frequent lapses into childishness, and sometimes even come with me—thanks for the cobweb candyfloss, Seb!